Augustin Daly, Franz von Schönthan

Seven-twenty-eight, or, Casting the Boomerang

A Comedy of Today in Four Acts

Augustin Daly, Franz von Schönthan

Seven-twenty-eight, or, Casting the Boomerang
A Comedy of Today in Four Acts

ISBN/EAN: 9783744782555

Printed in Europe, USA, Canada, Australia, Japan

Cover: Foto ©Andreas Hilbeck / pixelio.de

More available books at **www.hansebooks.com**

SEVEN-TWENTY-EIGHT

OR

CASTING THE BOOMERANG

A Comedy of To-Day, in Four Acts

(FROM THE GERMAN OF VON SCHÖNTHAN)

BY

AUGUSTIN DALY

As acted at Daly's Theatre for the first time, February 24, 1883

(Extract from Webster's Dictionary.)

BOOM-ER-ANG, *n.* A very singular missile weapon, used by the natives of Australia; when thrown from the hand, with a quick rotary motion, it describes very remarkable curves, according to the manner of throwing it, and finally taking a retrograde direction, so as to fall near the place from which it was thrown, or even very far in the rear of it. *In inexperienced hands the Boomerang recoils upon the thrower, sometimes with very serious results.*

FITZGERALD PUBLISHING CORPORATION
SUCCESSOR TO
DICK & FITZGERALD

18 Vesey St.,   New York

SEVEN-TWENTY-EIGHT.

DRAMATIS PERSONÆ AND ORIGINAL CAST.

COURTNEY CORLISS, *a gentleman of leisure, with a theory concerning boomerangs; employing his idle time in the pleasant pursuit of hunting a face,* MR. JOHN DREW.

MR. LAUNCELOT BARGISS, *a retired party who becomes the victim of the inevitable, and is bound, Mazeppa-like, to his wife's hobby* . . . MR. JAMES LEWIS.

PAUL HOLLYHOCK, *his son-in-law, devoted to his potato-beds until the Tempter comes.* . . . . MR. YORKE STEPHENS.

SIGNOR PALMIRO TAMBORINI, *late Maître de Ballet, Covent Garden, now on a mission and searching for an original* . . . . . MR. WILLIAM GILBERT.

A POSTMAN, ON HIS ROUND . . . . MR. E. T. WEBBER.

PROFESSOR GASLEIGH, *inventor and founder of a refuge for the outcasts of the pen* . . . . MR. CHARLES LECLERCQ.

JOBBINS, *Hollyhock's farmer* . . . . MR. W. H. BEEKMAN.

MRS. HYPATIA BARGISS, *a lady possessed of ancestors, aspirations, and a hobby.* . . . . MRS. G. H. GILBERT.

DORA HOLLYHOCK, *her daughter, with a grievance, and who becomes at once her husband's tempter and victim* . . . . MISS VIRGINIA DREHER.

FLOS, *the much sought "7-20-8"* . . . . MISS ADA REHAN.

JESSIE, *with yearnings beyond her station* . . . . . MISS HELEN LEYTON.

The action of the first and second acts passes at Bargiss's country place, somewhere in the Empire State.

The action of the third and fourth acts passes in the city near Central Park.

ACT I. — THE THEORY OF THE BOOMERANG. The Search is begun, and the "Scattered Leaflets" arrive.

ACT II. — THE SERPENT IN THE GARDEN. Serpent — Mr. Gasleigh. The boomerangs are cast.

ACT III. — INTOXICATION OF THE METROPOLIS. The Drama of the Missing Lamp and the Romance of the Forsaken! A novel illumination.

ACT IV. — THE BOOMERANG'S RETURN. His Lordship proposes, and Destiny is fulfilled.

TIME OF REPRESENTATION. — TWO HOURS AND A HALF.

CORLISS. Acts I. and II. — Fashionable summer suit (sack coat); straw hat. Act III. — Evening suit; overcoat; silk hat. Act IV. — Black cutaway coat and waistcoat; cassimere trousers; derby hat; overcoat; gloves.

BARGISS. Acts I., II., and III. — Trousers and waistcoat; dressing-gown. Flowing robe, long beard, and very tall hat, for "High Priest" costume at end of Act III. Act IV. — Ordinary morning suit (frock coat); overcoat; hat. He wears a half-bald gray wig, with whiskers to match.

HOLLYHOCK. Acts I. and II. — Soft felt hat; corduroy trousers tucked into farm boots; shooting-jacket. Act III. — Full evening dress, with outer garment for street; silk hat. "Conspirator's" dress to close Act III., big black cloak, broad-brimmed slouch hat, etc. Act IV. — Ordinary business suit.

TAMBORINI. Dress suit throughout; wears order in buttonhole; crush opera hat. Long linen duster only at 1st entrance, Act I. He wears a black curly wig, with mustache and imperial to correspond.

POSTMAN. Conventional postman's uniform, with cap. Waterproof cape in Act III.

GASLEIGH. Business suit, of a style several years behind the times, rather worn; rusty derby hat.

JOBBINS. The ordinary rig of a farm superintendent.

MRS. BARGISS. Act I. — Thin figured morning dress; summer hat, etc. Act II. — Same, without hat. Act III. — Home evening dress; cloak and hat for end of act. Act IV. — Street or travelling dress.

MRS. HOLLYHOCK. Acts I. and II. — Summer morning dress; no hat. Act III. — Handsome dinner or evening dress; wraps for street, etc. Act IV. — Morning gown.

FLOSSY. Acts I. and II. — Summer morning dress; hat, etc. Act III. — Home evening dress. Act IV. — Morning dress.

JESSIE. Neat muslin gown; linen collar and cuffs; lace cap.

PROPERTIES.

ACT I. — Table and chairs c. Sofa L. Chair up R. Other chairs placed conveniently about stage. Whistle, papers, and letter for POSTMAN. Cards, in case, and coins for CORLISS. An art catalogue. Large mastiff dog, and card, for FLOSSY. Letter (in envelope) and paper for MRS. HOLLYHOCK. Books on shelf R. Magazine for JESSIE. Spectacles, for BARGISS, on table c. Bell, lamp, and flowers in vase on table c. Carpet down. Whip for HOLLYHOCK.

ACT II. — Furniture, etc., as in Act I. Books, in basket, for MRS. BARGISS. Bust of Dante for JESSIE. Letters for MRS. HOLLYHOCK and CORLISS. Four pens and notebook for BARGISS. Document, in large wallet, for GASLEIGH. Envelope and paper for HOLLYHOCK. Manuscripts for BARGISS and MRS. BARGISS. Watches for CORLISS and TAMBORINI. Sandwich, glass of wine, and napkin for BARGISS. Sandwich, glass of wine, and handkerchief for GASLEIGH.

ACT III. — Shade and heavy curtains at window. Mirror R. Desk, chair, and revolving bookcase L. Books in bookcase. Papers, writing-materials, bust of Dickens, and two candelabra on desk. Bust of Shakespeare and two candelabra on mantel. Table and easy-chairs in front of mantel. Chandelier c. Divan c. Piano l. Chairs r., r. c., c., and r. of divan. Carpet down. Several books on table c. Artificial flowers for Jessie. Pair of shoes for Jessie to bring on. Cards, in case, and coin for Corliss. Candelabrum (not lighted) and some letters and papers for Jessie. Four pens for Bargiss. Large handbill for Hollyhock. Check for Bargiss. Several folded napkins, and some cracked ice in a bowl, for Jessie. Red book for Gasleigh. Student-lamp (not lighted) for Jessie. Book for Flossy. Letter for Mrs. Hollyhock. Bell on table c. Mrs. Bargiss's cloak and hat, for Jessie to bring on. Noise, rain, wind, thunder and lightning, off stage. Small shaded lamp (lighted) for Flossy. Door-bell off l. c. Whistle, mail-bag, and handkerchief for Postman. Matches on mantel. Coin, in pocket, for Flossy.

Act IV. — Furniture, etc., as in Act III. Card on salver for Jessie. Large bouquet, notebook and pencil, for Tamborini. Bolt inside door r. 3 e. Shawl up stage for Bargiss. Chair at door l. c. Letter and book for Mrs. Bargiss. Spectacles for Bargiss. Bargiss's hat and overcoat up stage. Rose in vase on piano. Large clothes-basket filled with books. Handkerchief for Bargiss. Eyeglasses for Mrs. Bargiss. An open and a sealed telegram for Tamborini.

ABBREVIATIONS.

In observing, the player is supposed to face the audience. c. means centre; r., right; l., left; r. c., right of centre; l. c., left of centre; c. d., centre door; r. d., right door; l. d., left door; d. r. c., door right of centre; d. l. c., door left of centre; d. f., door in the flat; c. d. f., centre door in the flat; r. d. f., right door in the flat; l. d. f., left door in the flat; 1 g., 2 g., 3 g., etc., first, second, or third grooves, etc.; 1 e., 2 e., 3 e., etc., first, second, or third entrances, etc.; r. u. e., right upper entrance; l. u. e., left upper entrance; up, up stage or toward the rear; down, down stage or toward the audience; x., means to cross the stage; x. r., cross toward the right; x. l., cross toward the left.

R.   R. C.   C.   L. C.   L.

SEVEN – TWENTY – EIGHT;

OR,

'CASTING THE BOOMERANG.

ACT I.

SCENE. — Vestibule or sitting-room in a comfortable country mansion. A chimneypiece C. *Bay-window at* L. C. *Archway and conservatory reached by two steps* R. C. *Doors* R. I E., R. 3 E., *and* L. 2 E. *Table and chairs* C. *Sofa* L. *The place has an old-fashioned but very homelike air. The curtain rises to the air of* "Wait for the Wagon." *The country* POSTMAN *appears at the bay-window,* L. C., *and gives his usual sharp whistle. He leans half through the half-open sash of the bay-window. ENTER* JESSIE *from* R. C. *READY* MRS. BARGISS, *to enter* R. C.

JESSIE (*a spry, neat maid-servant*). Coming, coming!

POSTMAN. Lively, then! (*Hands down papers and a letter.*) There you are.

JES. That all?

POSTMAN. Till next time. (*EXIT,* L. C.)

JES. (*coming forward and sorting the packages*). There's the *Tribune* for Mr. Bargiss, and the *Bazar* for Mrs. Bargiss, and — and the *Agriculturist* for Mr. Hollyhock, and one letter for Mrs. Hollyhock. What a sight of newspapers we do take in, and how few letters! But this place is out of the world.   Nobody wastes letters on us.   (*Lays the papers on table, and keeps the letter in her hand.*)

ENTER Mrs. Bargiss, *from conservatory*, R.C., *with summer hat, etc.   Middle-aged and sprightly.*

Mrs. Bargiss.   Has the post come, Jessie?

Jes.   Yes'm.   Nothing but one letter for Mrs. Hollyhock. (*Crosses to* R.)

Mrs. B. (*getting* L. *of table*).   And no papers?

Jes.   Oh, yes'm.   The regular lot come as usual.

Mrs. B. (*looking over papers at table*).   Wasn't there a magazine with them?   A new magazine with an old-gold cover?

Jes.   No'm.   Not as I see.

Mrs. B.   If the postman brings one, fetch it to me before anybody else sees it.

Jes.   Very well'm.

Mrs. B.   I expect it to-day.   You'll know it by the very peculiar color of its cover — a sort of orange or yellow.   Do you know what old-gold is?

[*READY* Corliss, *to enter* R. C.

Jes.   No'm.   I know what old silver and old greenbacks look like.

Mrs. B.   Well, it's like nothing you ever saw, then. You'll know it directly.

Jes.   Please'm, what's the name of it?

Mrs. B.   "Scattered Leaflets."   (*Crosses to* R.)   Can you remember the name?

Jes.   "Scattered Leaflets."   Oh, yes'm.

Mrs. B.   Don't forget, then — and bring it to me instantly.   (*EXIT,* R. *lower door.*)

Jes.   Yes'm.   Instantly.   I've heard that word before. They want everything instantly in this house.   (*Goes up and looks off through the bay-window,* L. C.)   My sakes! if there ain't a strange young gentleman coming up the walk — and coming right in, too! Well, he's cool! (*Retreats down* C.) Who knows — the beaux may be coming after Miss Flossy at last. Oh, I do hope and pray they be! It goes to my heart to see a young thing like her wasted on nobody, the way she is. (*Gets* L.)

ENTER CORLISS, R. C., *through the conservatory; looks about him and comes down.*

CORLISS (R.). Ah! (*Seeing* JESSIE.) I believe this is Mr. — Mr. — (*politely and evasively*).

JES. Mr. Bargiss's? Yes, sir. (*Aside.*) He's real nice — I hope he's a beau.

COR. Mr. Bargiss's — thank you — and Mrs. Bargiss's, of course?

JES. Yes, sir. There's Mrs. Bargiss, too. Shall I tell them, sir?

COR. Wait a moment.

JES. Oh, I can't, sir. I have no time.

COR. (*touching her chin*). What, so young — and "no time" already?

JES. (*crosses to* R.). Oh, Mr. Bargiss gets in an awful temper if he sees any of us idling.

COR. Bargiss must be a tyrant. Not the least like the smiling visage that beams upon us from this silver dollar, eh? (*Gives her a piece of money.*)

JES. I'll compare the likeness when I see him. (*Pockets it.*)

COR. Now, answer me a question. (*Takes a card from his pocket.*) Look at this. It's a crest, you perceive — a shield with a two-headed —

JES. A two-headed goose on it.

COR. A double-headed swan. Tell me, have you ever seen a crest like that anywhere?

JES. (R.). I thought it was a goose. Why, Missis has that on her notepaper and envelopes.

COR. Your mistress?

JES. Yes — *old* Missis.

COR. Old — how old?

JES. I guess she's near fifty.

COR. That's sufficient. (*Puts up card, disappointed. Going up* R.)

JES. I guess she thinks it's sufficient, too. (*Going.*)

COR. (*pauses*). Stop a moment. (R. *Comes back.*) Tell me, are there any other ladies in the family?

JES. Oh, yes. There's the two daughters. One's married to Mr. Hollyhock — and the other is Miss Flossy.

COR. (*interested*). Miss Flossy? Young?

JES. Oh, yes.

COR. How young?

JES. Eighteen.

COR. Pause there. Does she own a very large dog?

JES. (*quickly*). Oh, yes. Max.

COR. Now, look at this picture attentively. (*Produces an art catalogue.*) It's the illustrated catalogue of the Academy for '82. Page 32. No. 728. "Portrait of a Lady." Do you know the young lady?

JES. Why, it's Miss Flos and Max.

COR. (*replaces the pamphlet and seizes her hand, producing from his pocket another coin*). If I ask you to swear by this image of our bright Goddess of Liberty not to mention my inquiries to any one, will you do so?

JES. Do you intend to stop and see the family?

COR. I came for that purpose.

JES. (*crosses to* R.). Then I won't say a word unless I find I ought to, you know.

COR. Of course. Is it a bargain?

JES. Yes, sir. (*Pockets the coin, and aside, in a flutter of delight.*) He's come after Miss Flos along of her portrait.

Oh, how romantic! I wouldn't spoil it for the world. (*Looking off*, L. C.) Look! There's Miss Flossy, her own self, in the garden now. Shall I go and tell her you're here?

COR. By no means. I shall introduce myself to her father.

JES. Yes, sir. I'll tell Mr. Bargiss at once. (*Going; aside.*) Oh, ain't it romantic, and just too lovely! (*EXIT, R. C., with letter.*)

[*READY* FLOSSY, *with mastiff, to enter* R. C.

COR. (*steps to window*, L. C.). How's this? How's this? The young lady is a distinct blonde, and the portrait at the Academy is that of a brunette. She looks this way. The same eyes. What a pair of eyes! I recognize the eyes. Heavenly! Now she looks again. I have found her at last. (*Comes down.*) And now that I have found her, what of it, my boy? Is it worth my while to come on this expedition? I see a picture — I fall in love — and I act like a fool. Rush on to danger without counting the cost. (*Sits on sofa*, L.) Let us look at this thing calmly. If a man wants to buy a watch, how carefully he examines it before purchasing. It must be real gold, admirable as to manufacture, thoroughly tested and perfect as a timekeeper. We call for a guaranty, take it on trial, and return it if it doesn't go. All this trouble for a watch. (FLOSSY *appears passing window, leading a large mastiff.*) When it comes to a wife, who guarantees the genuineness of the metal? How are we to know about the works in her? (*Taps his heart.*) Who'll take her back if she doesn't go, or goes too fast? (*Rising.*) Conclusion: Be on your guard, my boy — be on — ah, here she is! (*Salutes* FLOSSY *very respectfully as she ENTERS from grounds*, R. C., *through the conservatory, in morning dress, hat, etc.*) Good-morning, Miss — Miss —

FLOSSY (R.). Good-morning. (*Distantly.*) Are you waiting for papa?

COR. Not exactly.

FLOS. No? Oh I It's my brother-in-law, Mr. Hollyhock? (*Going a step to* R.)

COR. Not quite that, either.

FLOS. (*puts dog off* R. 1 D.). Oh, then — (*going*).

COR. Then *what* do I want? I see you are naturally
curious to —

FLOS. (*towards him*). Not at all — but we so seldom see
anybody here — it's quite an event when we have a call.
We live in such seclusion.

COR. I really sympathize with you.

FLOS. It's quite a humiliating confession, isn't it —
to acknowledge I find it dull? I ought to have all sorts
of resources; all well-bred young ladies are supposed to
have.

COR. (L.). Utter nonsense I Seclusion is very well for
age; to youth it is a prison. The glare of the ballroom is
for a young girl what the sunlight is for the flower.

FLOS. Please tell my father and brother-in-law that.
They won't believe *me*.

COR. I shall certainly do so. In the meantime, permit
me to tell you what brought me here, and ask your sym-
pathy and aid. I heard that the neighborhood contained a
hidden treasure.   [*She looks at him, amazed.*
Let us say, for instance, a celebrated piece of tapestry —
or a rare bit of china — which I am anxious to possess.

FLOS. It's quite interesting.

COR. You find it so? Thank you. I thought you would.
I wish to keep the matter secret for the present, and I need
some pretext for remaining just long enough to examine my
treasure before making an offer.

FLOS. That seems reasonable.

COR. You find it so? Thank you. I thought you would.
I have brought a letter of introduction to your father.

FLOS. (*going up* R.). I left him in the garden.

COR. (*getting* R.). Thanks. Permit me one word.

Flos. (*turns down* L.). Certainly.

Cor. Thank you again. I thought you would. This letter will not insure me more than half an hour's stay in this house. What can I do after that?

Flos. (L.). Call again to-morrow.

Cor. No. I want a good excuse for staying, and I am a poor hand at forcing an acquaintance.

Flos. (L., *mischievously*). You don't do yourself justice.

Cor. That means you think me rather impudent.

Flos. (*self-possessed*). Rather imprudent. Suppose I were to reveal your plans to the lord of the manor?

Cor. You won't do that. In fact, I dare to count upon your assistance.

[*READY* Mrs. Hollyhock, *with letter, to enter*
R. 3 D.

Flos. Why, I don't even know you.

Cor. And yet you would trust me. In fact, you trust me already. For the present, content yourself with my honest face and — my name. (*Hands her his card.*)

Flos. It will end in your getting me into a scrape. I don't want to be found out in anything foolish.

Cor. Anything foolish? My dear young lady, have you ever listened to old people when they talk among themselves? Do so! You will find that the dearest recollections of their youth are the follies they committed. They are the evergreens in the wreaths of memory. I beg of you, then, don't neglect to lay in a stock for your old age. Do something *now* to laugh over heartily *then*. You can do nothing wiser. Come, then! Just one little good-natured folly to begin with. Keep my secret. Thank you. I thought you would. I'll go and find your father. Remember, when we meet again, forget that we have met before. *Au revoir.* (*EXIT*, R. C.)

Flos. (*sees him off; then comes down*). That's the first person I've seen in six months that I could speak a sensible word with. (*Reads card.*) "Courtney Corliss." Isn't it strange that nice-looking people always have such pretty names.

ENTER Mrs. HOLLYHOCK, R. 3 D., *with a letter.*

MRS. HOLLYHOCK (R.). Here's a letter for you, Flos. It came enclosed to me. (*Takes letter from envelope and throws envelope carelessly on table* C.; *comes down* L.)

FLOS. (*crosses to* R., *looking at signature*). It's from Mr. Palette, the painter.

MRS. H. (L.). Unfortunately.

FLOS. Why so?

MRS. H. Candidly, I blame myself in this matter. We met him at Nahant last fall, and he painted your portrait.

FLOS. Mamma knew about it, and was present at all the sittings.

MRS. H. Yes, but papa knew nothing about it. We shouldn't have allowed Mr. Palette to send it to the Academy. I tremble to think what papa and, worst of all, my husband, would say if they knew your portrait was on exhibition.

FLOS. (R.). They needn't know. We've kept it secret so far.

MRS. H. Who knows how much longer we can do so? There! (*Produces a paper.*) There's a notice of it in the papers already.

FLOS. (*delight*). Of my picture?

MRS. H. Listen. (*Reads.*) "The gem among the portraits is No. 728. A young girl seated, with a gigantic mastiff at her feet. The artist persistently refuses to disclose the original of his charming picture."

FLOS. Well, you see he is discreet.

MRS. H. Wait. (*Reads.*) "Yet there is a trifling circumstance which might give an ardent admirer a clew to the mystery. On the embroidered *fichu* worn by the lady there appears, among heraldic arabesques, the figure of a two-headed swan."

FLOS. (R.). Mamma's crest!

MRS. H. Yes. The double-headed swan of mamma's very distant if not apocryphal English ancestors. Suppose papa should read that article —

FLOS. But, Dora, the whole thing's so harmless. I'm sure I'm not in love with Mr. Palette. He vowed it would make his reputation if I sat, with Max, for a picture — and I didn't want to crush him at the outset of his career. It was very flattering, and I felt like his muse. Some day, when he gets into the " Encyclopædia of Painters," it will be mentioned that his first successful picture was a portrait of Miss Florence Bargiss — and so I'll get into the Encyclopædia too, and be immortal with him. (*Crosses to* L.)

MRS. H. (R.). Well, if you get in there, my husband will get a divorce.

FLOS. That's because he's an awful prig, and appreciates nothing but sheep and pigs.

MRS. H. (*sighs*). Unhappily. Well, what does your painter say in his letter?

[*READY* HOLLYHOCK, *with whip, to enter* R. C.

FLOS. (*laughs*). I forgot all about the letter. (*Reads.*) "Dear Miss Bargiss, — Your portrait has made a sensation. I had a quite singular experience with it, however. When it was finished, I became sensible that your face lacked a certain indispensable expression." Well, I declare! "There was a certain something, unfortunately, very commonplace about it, which I tried in vain to idealize." (*Furious.*) Upon my word!

MRS. H. Candid, I must say.

FLOS. (*reads,* L.). "At last I tried the effect of substituting for your own hair, which is of the ordinary blonde type, and worn too severely, a mass of rich, dark curls. The effect was magical. The likeness, it is true, suffered greatly,

but, from an artistic standpoint"— (*Throws the letter down.*)
I could cry with vexation. (*Up.*)

MRS. H. (*crossing to* L.; *picks up letter*). I should say so!

FLOS. (R.). And I was so proud — I thought — oh !

MRS. H. (*soothingly*). There — don't waste a thought
more on it.   [FLOSSY *bounds away from her, to* L.

ENTER HOLLYHOCK, R. C., *in farm boots and shooting-jacket,*
carrying a whip.

HOLLYHOCK (R.). I say, Dora, I wanted — (*stops*).
What's the matter? Have you two been quarrelling?

MRS. H. (*crossing to* C.). No, no.

HOL. What letter is that?

MRS. H. Nothing important.

                    [*READY* MRS. BARGISS, *to enter* R. I D.

HOL. Let me see it.

MRS. H. (*crossing to* L., *pockets letter*). Don't be in-
quisitive.

HOL. (*to* FLOSSY). You've been crying.

FLOS. (*crossing to* R., *pettishly*). Well, I know I have.

HOL. What for?

FLOS. Because I'm unhappy. Because I'm kept here
secluded and imprisoned like a nun.

HOL. Hol-lo!

FLOS. And because I'm bored to death. (R.) If you
don't want a young girl to die of the blues, you must give
her something to amuse her. The glare of the ballroom is
what I want. The flowers pine for the sunlight — so do I.
(*Stage* R.)

HOL. (C.). There's lots of sunlight here. I get on
amazingly.

FLOS. (*up to him*). You! You are laying up a nice old
age for yourself! I don't believe you ever committed a
folly in your life. Where will your memories come from —
where are *your* evergreens? (*EXIT*, R. I D.)

HOL. I don't comprehend. What's the matter with her?
MRS. H. Oh, it's some freak. Goodness knows what she thinks about.

[READY BARGISS *and* CORLISS, *to enter* R. C.

ENTER MRS. BARGISS, R. 1 D., *looking back after* FLOSSY.

MRS. BARGISS (*crossing to* C.). Dora, has the postman brought anything for me yet?   [PAUL *saunters up* R.
MRS. H. Not that I know of, mamma.
MRS. B. I wish you would ask about the place. There must be something.
MRS. H. I will, mamma. (*EXIT,* R. C.)
MRS. B. It's unaccountable. (*Goes to bay-window,* L. C.)
[HOLLYHOCK *looks after* DORA, *and comes down.*
HOL. (*looking on the table, has found the envelope that* DORA *threw down, which he examines carefully*). There is something in the wind. Flossy crying, and Dora hiding a letter from me. This must be the envelope. Postmarked New York, and addressed to my wife. (*Forward.*) In a man's handwriting. I say, mother, do you know Dora's correspondent in New York?
MRS. B. (L. C., *at window ; not turning*). No. Why do you ask?
HOL. (*evasively*). Nothing in particular. (*Aside.*) She shall tell me whom that letter is from. (*Pockets envelope.*) There's father yonder. I wonder if he knows.

BARGISS *appears at back, in conservatory, in dressing-gown, with* CORLISS. *They stop in conversation.*

BARGISS. Ah! There's Hollyhock, now. He'll give you the information, no doubt. (*Calls.*) Paul ! One moment !
HOL. Certainly. (*Goes up.*)
[BARGISS, *in pantomime, introduces* CORLISS *to him, and instructs him to show* CORLISS *over the grounds. They go off together, and* BARGISS *comes down.*

Mrs. B. (*at window*, L. C., *speaking as* Paul *goes up*).   I hope the postman hasn't dropped the "Scattered Leaflets" on his way.   If it doesn't arrive to-day, I'll telegraph to the publisher.   This suspense is becoming unendurable.

Bar. (R.).   Ah, Hypatia!   There you are.   What are you doing at the window?

Mrs. B.   I'm waiting for the mail.

Bar.   Oh, it'll come in time.   Small loss if it doesn't. Nothing in the papers.

Mrs. B. (*meaningly*).   Perhaps there may be this time.

Bar. (*surprised*).   Why — what's going on?

Mrs. B. (L.).   Something that concerns me — deeply. Something that ought to concern you — and I hope it will.

Bar.   Go on, Hypatia; let's know all about it.

Mrs. B.   I intend it as a surprise — and yet it may be better to prepare you.

Bar.   You surprise me already.   Go on and prepare me fully.

Mrs. B. (*earnestly*).   Launcelot, how often have I told you how much it has pained me to see you wasting your time and talents in idleness?

Bar. (R.).   Idleness, my dear?   I get up at five every morning.

Mrs. B.   And go to bed at nine, as obscure — as unknown — as poor and as small as you got up.

Bar.   Hypatia!

Mrs. B. (*interrupting him, and with a lofty air*).   And you were made for something better and greater, Launcelot.

Bar.   Are you getting on that old subject again?   (*Crosses to* L. *and sits on sofa.*)

Mrs. B. (L. C.).   You are simply neglecting your duty and burying your talents.

Bar.   Whew — w!   (*Sits down* L.)

Mrs. B.   Look at what you have done — your writings — your poetry —

BAR. Now, my dear— (*Rising.*)

MRS. B. (*replacing him back*). You won't talk me out of it this time. There *is* something great in you. Your pen, in days gone by, flowed with inspiration.

BAR. (*on sofa*, L.). I confess I used to waste ink writing stuff I thought was poetry. Before I married you, I sinned largely in that respect. Stuff, my dear— all stuff— and poor stuff, too. I'm ashamed of it. (*Crosses to* R.)

MRS. B. Stuff? Your verses to me when we were engaged? Never! I read them over the other day, and they brought tears to my eyes.

BAR. (R.). You don't mean to say you kept that rubbish!

MRS. B. (*lachrymose*). Every line you ever wrote. In my desk. But that's not the place for them. They belong to the world.

BAR. (R.). That's what I thought thirty years ago, when I sent them to the magazines.

MRS. B. And they were declined with thanks. It's the fate of all unknown authors. Thank goodness, there's a change now. (*Strides proudly to* L.)

BAR. (*looking after her*). A change now— how?

MRS. B. Professor Gasleigh has started a new magazine.

BAR. Gasleigh? Never heard of him.

MRS. B. What of that? He never heard of *you.* Yet you are somebody— so's he.

[*READY* FLOSSY, *with card, and* JESSIE, *to enter*
R. C.

BAR. Excuse me—

MRS. B. His magazine is called "Scattered Leaflets." It is started to introduce unknown genius. He distinctly announces in his prospectus that he wants no contributions from so-called celebrities. He proposes to publish the efforts of his subscribers only.

BAR. (R.). Oh! Very good dodge. (*Crosses to* L.)

MRS. B. I have subscribed to the magazine, and sent him a collection of your fragments. I expect the magazine containing them to-day.

BAR. I *hope* he sends your bundle back unprinted.

MRS. B. He won't. He knows a good thing when he's got it.

BAR. That's what I'm afraid of.

MRS. B. What's that?

BAR. Never mind. I don't want to see the paper. Don't bring it to me. (*Up.*)

MRS. B. But, Launcelot!

BAR. I won't look at it. I won't have anything to do with it. I don't want to be roasted by those press fellows at my age.   [*READY* TAMBORINI, *to enter* R. C.

FLOSSY *appears, with* JESSIE, *at* R. C.

FLOSSY (*looking at a card she holds in her hand*). Papa, look at this. (*Sends* JESSIE *off.*)

MRS. B. (*eagerly*). Has it come?

FLOS. Who?

MRS. B. (*gets* C.). The "Scattered Leaflets."

FLOS. No; but a gentleman wants to see papa, and has sent his card with this written on it.

BAR. (*down, feeling for spectacles*). Where are my spectacles? Read it.

FLOS. (*reads*). "Signor Palmiro Romano Giovanni Tamborini," and he's written in pencil, "Formerly *Maitre de Ballet de* Covent Garden; now commissioned on behalf of Lord Lawntennis."

BAR. (*crosses to* R.; *takes card*). What's all that? What does he want?

FLOS. I don't know, papa, unless you've had some transactions with the Ballet in London,

[BARGISS *turns away, confused.*

or with Lord Lawntennis.

MRS. B. (L.) Signor Tamborini! He must be an Italian.

FLOS. (L.). Of course. [JESSIE *ushers in* TAMBORINI.

TAMBORINI *appears*, R. C., *in a long duster, under which is a dress suit — order in buttonhole — opera hat. He takes off duster and hands it to* JESSIE. *She puts it on chair, and EXIT*, R. C.

TAMBORINI (*shuts his hat and looks at his attire*). All right. (*Comes down* R. C. *with measured dancing-step. Bows grandly, pressing his hat with both hands against his left breast, and then extending it to arm's length. First addressing* MRS. BARGISS.) Signora! (*To* FLOSSY.) Signorina! (*To* BARGISS.) Signor!

BAR. (C.). Good-morning.

TAM. (R. C., *with strong accent and much gesture*). I beg a thousand pardons if I make a mistake in the language —

BAR. Oh, we'll understand one another.

MRS. B. Unfortunately, we don't speak Italian.

TAM. That is no matter, Signora. (*Profound bow*.) I know a little English, and if I can't think of a word, I know how to help myself out. I have been Master of the Ballet at the Royal Opera for twenty years. If a word sticks in my stupid head (*gesture*), or my stupid tongue (*gesture*), I make it out with my hand (*gesture*). If I want to say *Te voglio bene*, I do *so*. (*Makes ballet-gesture of loving.*)

FLOS. (L.). Oh! So that means love?

TAM. (*applauds*). Bravo, Signorina! Then when I want to say *Sposare*, I do *so*. (*Gesture of proposing in marriage.*)

MRS. B. You are proposing marriage. It's quite plain.

TAM. *Divorzo*, I do *so*. (*Gesture of taking wedding-ring from his finger and throwing it away.*)

BAR. Ah! Divorce! Just so! That's very plain, too. Ah, there's a great deal that's very plain in the ballet. I always liked the ballet. Especially Taglioni — ah, what a dancer she was! (*With enthusiasm.*)

TAM. Oh, oh, oh, oh !   Signor, do not say that !   (*Gesture of negative with hand.*)   Old school — old style !   You should see our *Prima Ballerina* in *Milano*.   Oh, oh !   (*Gesture of ecstasy.*)   La Braggazetta.   She is an *artiste*.   Ah !   (*Throws kisses with both hands.*)   With Taglioni art was small — *so*. (*Indicates a few inches from his hand.*)   But the puffs were big — *so !* (*Opens both arms.*)   With Braggazetta, the puffs are small — *so*. (*Indicates about an inch from the floor.*)   But the art — *so !* (*In his ecstasy, he pulls up the nearest chair, stands on it, and indicates the height of art with his hat in his upheld hand.   Instantly seeing his impropriety, he descends. Bowing with effusion.*)   Ladies, I beg (*gesture*) for pardon. Pardon me.   When I speak of my art I always lose my head. (*About to replace the chair.*)

MRS. B.   If you please, keep the chair, and be seated.

TAM.   If you allow me, I'll take the liberty.   (*Takes chair and offers it quickly to* MRS. BARGISS, *who declines and sits on sofa.   He offers it to* FLOSSY, *who declines and stands by her mother.   He offers it to* BARGISS, *who sits with a grunt.   Then finally he takes his own chair, and, after looking to see if the others are seated, sits, himself, with a pompous pose.*)

BAR.   (*looks at card*).   You are commissioned on behalf of Lord Lawntennis —

TAM.   Si, Signor —

BAR.   Yes, I see.

TAM.   And I have called by his Lordship's command, to ask you a most submissive question.   (*Bows.*)

BAR. ´ What is it ?

TAM.   His lordship is a fool (*general surprise; gesture and checks himself*) on the subject of art.   He comes to travel in America.   He sees at the Academy National of Design the portrait of a young and beautiful lady (*gesture*) with a big — big (*gesture of size*) dog.

FLOS.   (*alarmed, aside to* MRS. BARGISS).   Mamma !

MRS. B.   (*same*).   Sh !

TAM. His lordship say to me, "Palmiro," he say to me, "I am anxious to know who the handsome young lady in the portrait is and where she lives. But the artist gives no information. Therefore, search, Palmiro! Like a hunter to the hounds. *Avanti!* Seek! Seek, Palmiro! (*Pantomime of hounds on scent, but not leaving his chair.*)

BAR. Well, did you find the young lady?

TAM. Ah, *Dio mio*, Signor! That was not so easy. But Palmiro is cunning fellow. I seek here — I seek there — and finally, right in the corner of the picture — what you think — I see a date. Nahant, 1881 — Nahant! (*Gesture.*) That is a watering-place. (*Makes figures in the air with his fingers.*) 1881! That is a clew. Oh, what a head I have! I go by train to Boston — to Nahant. (*Gesture and sound of train.*) I ask the big people (*gesture*) and the little people (*gesture*).

MRS. B. And did you learn the young lady's name?

TAM. No, Signora; but I learned the young lady who was portrayed (*gesture*) was the daughter of a gentleman — who live in this place.

BAR. (*starts up*). In this place! (*To* MRS. BARGISS.) You were at Nahant last year.

MRS. B. (*rises*). Why, my dear, you don't for one moment suppose —

FLOS. (L. C.; *all rise*). Do you think it was I, papa? (*Archly.*)

TAM. (R. C.; *quickly*). No, no! The Signorina is not the original. The lady in the picture has quite a different head of hair. All dark — all curls —

FLOS. (*helping him*). Curls like that, eh?

TAM. Si, Signorina. *Grazia tanto.*

BAR. Then it can't be Dora, either.

FLOS. Of course not.

TAM. So? That is bad. (*Shakes his head sadly.*)

BAR. I beg your pardon, it's not bad at all. It wouldn't

suit me to have my daughters sit for artists' models. We don't allow such things in this country, Signor.

MRS. B. (L.). Certainly not. (*Crosses to* TAMBORINI.)

TAM. *Ma Dio mio.* What will I do ! *Adesso !*

BAR. You can inquire in the neighborhood. There are plenty of fools in it.

FLOS. (*crosses close to him*). I think Mrs. Van Horn has a niece with black hair. She wears it in ringlets.

TAM. *Da Vero !* Ah, Signorina, you take a stone from my heart. (*Gesture to* BARGISS.) *Grazia tanto,* Signor. (*Going up* C.) I run *stante pede* to the neighbor. (*Turns at arch.*) What is their name ?

BAR. Van Horn. Horn. (*Action of taking a drink.*) It's the next house but two.

TAM. *Ah, Capisca !* Mr. Van Horn. (*Gesture of blowing.*) Horn — that is easily remembered. *Adio,* Signor — Signora — Signorina — *Complimenti Signore.* (*EXIT, quickly,* R. C.)

> [*READY* CORLISS *and* MRS. HOLLYHOCK, *to enter*
> R. C.

MRS. B. (L., *aside*). Thank goodness !

BAR. The fellow's a regular jumping-jack — but what a scare he gave me ! If one of you girls had been so foolish as to get yourself painted for show — I'd — you know how I hate this rushing into public. (*Goes up irritated, and walks about.*)

MRS. B. (*crosses to* C.). Now, Launcelot —

FLOS. (L.). O mamma, what a pity it is we can't tell him !

MRS. B. Don't bother me, you great baby. (*Up.*)

FLOS. It's pretty good for a baby to have a lord fall in love with her picture. (*Crosses to* R.)

BAR. (*suddenly comes down* R. *of table ; and taking up a magazine, pitches it aside*). It's too bad !

MRS. B. What ails you now ?

[FLOSSY *looks at books on shelf* R.

BAR. I can't get your "Scattered Leaflets" out of my head. Which of my poems did you send him, anyway?

MRS. B. "The Pansy Chain."

BAR. (*reflectively*). Hum! Hum! They are not so very bad, fortunately. Particularly that "Sonnet to the Moonbeam Shining on my True Love's Eyelid!" (*Suddenly.*) Why the deuce doesn't the confounded magazine come? The suspense and uncertainty make me nervous. (*Walks about.*)

CORLISS *appears at* R. C. *with* MRS. HOLLYHOCK.

MRS. B. Sh!

CORLISS. Pardon me for disturbing you again. Your son-in-law bade me wait for him here.

[FLOSSY *is next to* DORA, R.

BAR. Certainly! Certainly! Mrs. Bargiss — my wife. My daughter (*introducing*), Mr. Corliss. Thinks of settling in our vicinity. Tired of the city.

MRS. B. Tired of New York?

FLOS. Are you a New Yorker?   [CORLISS *bows.*

BAR. New York! New York! It's the old song! I'm pestered to death by those women every day to leave a quiet, decent, healthy country home and crowd into a great barracks they call New York.

MRS. B. (L.). An owl's nest. We are mouldering into dust here.

BAR. Don't let them frighten you, my young friend. You'll do capitally here. Look at me. I've sat in the owl's nest twenty years. Am I mouldering into dust? I've had my day in the city, and now I've settled down to rest.

FLOS. But papa — we haven't had *our* day in the city.

MRS. B. Time enough to rest when you have achieved something.

BAR. You must know, Mr. Corliss, that my wife has a

hobby. She wants me to be somebody. As if it wasn't enough, at the close of one's life, to say, " I've been a decent fellow. I've never wronged any one. And never made a fool of myself."

COR. (*calmly*). Very high praise — if you deserve it.

BAR. (*hesitating*). Well — so far, I've never done anything *particularly* foolish.

COR. So much the worse.

BAR. Why so much the worse ?

COR. Because you've got it to do.

[*READY* JESSIE, *with a magazine, to enter* R. C.

BAR. Allow me —

COR. Pardon me. I mean no reflection. I simply state a fact. Every one commits, at some period of his life, a signal act of folly — takes a step and stumbles — makes an effort that recoils upon his head — throws, in fact, a boomerang that returns to floor him. It's destiny. No one escapes.

MRS. B. There must be exceptions.

COR. (*crosses to* L.; *politely*). I fear not, madame. To speak figuratively, folly sits enthroned above us in the clouds, smiling at our efforts to be wise, and confident that the time must come when we forget our sense, our wit, our wisdom and experience, and cast our little boomerang.

MRS. B. (R.). And may we inquire whether you yourself have —

COR. (*smiles*). I ? Oh, I propitiate the goddess by half a dozen small follies every day.

BAR. Well, my young friend, I believe as little in your theory as in your goddess. I have survived the years of folly, and would particularly like to see the temptation that would induce me to commit one.

ENTER JESSIE, R. C., *holding a magazine aloft in her hand.*

JESSIE. Here it is at last !

Bar. (*at arch*). What, what?

Jes. The "Scattered Leaflets."

Mrs. B. (*runs before him, snatches it from* Jessie, *and tears the wrapper off*). At last we shall know. Remember my words, Launcelot. [*EXIT* Jessie, R. C.

Bar. (L. *of* Mrs. Bargiss, *excited*). Never mind! Get it open! It's really too silly, but I am curious to know.

Mrs. B. (*has opened the pamphlet; screams*). Launcelot!

Bar. Well! Well!

Mrs. B. You are in it! (*Falls on his neck.*)

Mrs. H.) (*together*). Mamma!
Flos.) What *is* the matter?

Mrs. B. My children, see! Your father's in print. (*Crosses between the two girls and back.*)

Mrs. H. *and* Flos. Where? How?

Mrs. B. (*reads proudly*). "The Pansy Chain, by Launcelot Bargiss." (*Crosses to* R.)

Bar. (*looks over book, reads line and repeats, swelling with pride and pleasure*). By Launcelot Bargiss! By Launcelot Bargiss! Allow me to look at it. I should think it interested the author quite as much as anybody. Where the deuce are my spectacles? Have any of you girls — (*Stage*, R. C., *takes it pompously.* Flossy *gets his glasses from the table. He puts them on and looks over the magazine.*) It's really there. Ha, ha, ha! (*Quiet laugh of pleasure.*) "The Pansy Chain, by Launcelot Bargiss." By Launcelot Bargiss — that's your dad. [*READY* Jessie, *to enter* R. C.

Flos. (*crosses, embraces her father and mother hastily but fervently, turns with open arms to* Corliss — *checks herself suddenly*). Oh, papa is in the papers at last! (*Crosses to* Corliss.)

Mrs. B. He may thank me for it.

Bar. The types actually dance up and down before my eyes. It's really ridiculous; but to see one's self in print for the first time —

COR. (*politely, crosses to* L. C.). So your husband is an author?

MRS. B. (*suddenly reserved, and nudging* BARGISS). Ye—es. He sent a trifle for this number. The editors are so persistent.

COR. I understood it was his first—

MRS. B. Oh, no—he's been writing for years. (*Crosses to* L. C.)

BAR. (*tapping his forehead*). And the well's not quite dry yet.

FLOS. Do let us see, papa. (*Crosses to* C.)

COR. And may I have the pleasure—

BAR. (*airily*). Oh, if it interests you, I should be glad to give you a copy. (*To* MRS. BARGISS.) Have we—a—any more?   [*READY* TAMBORINI, *to enter* R. C.

MRS. B. (*touching bell*). Possibly—I—don't know.

ENTER JESSIE, R. C.

Ask at the store if they have any more "Scattered Leaflets."
    [DORA *crosses to* CORLISS *and* FLOSSY.

BAR. If not, tell them to send for half a dozen—or say a dozen—or two dozen of the—a—magazine, regularly.

JESSIE (*going*). Yes, sir.

BAR. Ah—and—a—tell the man to send for fifty of this number. No. 10. Tell him to be sure it's the number with the poems by Mr. Bargiss—Launcelot Bargiss—that's me.

JES. (*open mouth*). Yes, sir. (*EXIT,* R. C.)

FLOS. (*who has been reading*). Why, they are splendid, papa! Particularly the third one. (*Crosses next to* BARGISS, *and gives him book.*)

BAR. (*holds her hand to his shoulder, caressing her*). Do you think so? My dear, I always said our Flos knew a good thing—when she saw it.

MRS. B. The seventh is my favorite. It's beautiful

BAR. (*throws his arm round* FLOSSY'S *neck*). Hypatia ! (*Takes her hand.*)

MRS. B. I'll read it. Give me the book.

BAR. Not in presence of the author !

RE-ENTER TAMBORINI, *in archway,* R. C.

TAMBORINI. Pardon !

ALL (*backs to audience*). Hush !

TAM. I wanted to ask —

BAR. Sh ! My wife is going to read — a — something.

MRS. B. Yes. A poem of my husband's.

BAR. Printed in the Magazine ! *Comprenny ?*

MRS. B. (*clearing her throat, etc.*). It is called " Flowers Culled by the Wayside."

TAM. (R.). Ah ! *Capisco !* Flowers — culled — picked — pulled — (*gesture*) by Signor ! (*Points to* BARGISS.) Good ! Bravo !

MRS. B. (*to* FLOSSY *and* DORA, *who are chatting with* COR-LISS). Silence, if you please. .

ENTER JESSIE, R. C.

JESSIE (*entering and blurting out*). If you please, sir —

[BARGISS *runs her out,* R. C., *she struggling.*

Sir, if you please, sir —

BAR. Now, my dear —

ALL (*as above*). Hush !

[BARGISS *stands with his eyeglasses in his hand, beating time and looking smilingly at dome.* TAM-BORINI *accompanies the lines with gestures. The girls and* CORLISS *group down* L. MRS. BARGISS *stands* R. C. *and reads. All mark time.*

MRS. B. (*reads*).

" Once—as evening shadows fell,
    I sought my true love's door ;
    Then and there my vow was spoken
    To love her evermore."

COR. (*sotto voce*).   Bravo!   Bravo!
ALL.   Hush!
BAR. (*loftily*).   Another stanza!
MRS. B. (*reads*).

> "Ah, what was the song she sang to me,
> My sweet love at her door,
> While eyes and hearts were meeting,
> To love me evermore?"   (*Dries her eyes.*)

FLOS.   Sweet!   [*READY curtain.*
COR.   Capital!
MRS. H.   Beautiful.

TAM.   Bravo!   Bravo!   (*Seizes flowers from vase on table and crowns* BARGISS.)

BAR. (*seizes the magazine from his wife's hand and gazes at it rapturously as his wife embraces him*).   Yes — I am — I am a poet!

[*RING curtain.   The group breaks as the*

CURTAIN   FALLS.

ACT II.

SCENE. — Same as last. MRS. BARGISS *is discovered* R.,
placing books, which she takes from a basket, into bookcase.
ENTER JESSIE, R. C., *with a bust of Dante on her arm.*
READY MRS. HOLLYHOCK, *with letter, to enter* R. C.

JESSIE (R. C.). Please'm, I've washed all the dirt off
this old lady. Where shall I put her?

MRS. BARGISS (R.). Old lady! What an idea! That's
Dante — a celebrated poet.

JES. Lor'm, I thought it was an old woman, on account
of the hood and nightgown.

        [*READY* CORLISS *and* FLOSSY, *to enter* R. I D.

MRS. B. Put him on the table. Here. (*Assists* JESSIE
by removing lamp from table and placing it on mantel.) It
will give a literary air to the room. Take that basket away,
now.   [*EXIT* JESSIE, *with basket,* R. C.

ENTER MRS. HOLLYHOCK, R. C., *with a letter.*

MRS. HOLLYHOCK. This is really too bad!

MRS. B. What is?

MRS. H. Paul won't be home to dinner. He's going
away directly after luncheon, to the mill.

MRS. B. (*at bookcase*). Hum!

MRS. H. (L.). That's the way it is all the time. I don't
see my own husband any more. Up at five o'clock and off
to the fields. Stays all day, and falls asleep over his supper.
I'd like to know what I married for. (*Sits* R. *of table.*)

MRS. B. You should have listened to me. I warned you
about marrying a man who hadn't a single literary taste.

Mrs. H. (*seeing her error — rises*). Never mind. Don't say anything against him, mamma. I was wrong to complain. He loves me. I'll make it all right with him when he comes in. (*EXIT* R. 3 D.)

Mrs. B. Ah! It's all she can do, poor thing.

[*Goes to door* L., *and peeps in as*

Corliss *and* Flossy *ENTER at* R. 1 D.

Flossy (*advances to* Mrs. Bargiss). There's mamma now. Mr. Corliss is going away, mamma.

Corliss (R.). I have to thank you and your husband, madam, for the very great hospitality you have shown a stranger.

Mrs. B. (*crosses to* C.). Don't mention it, I beg. We had better not disturb Mr. Bargiss just now. He's composing. I'll tell him. (*EXIT* L. D.)

Flos. (L.). Ever since papa saw his poems in the paper, he's been another man. He keeps writing day and night.

Cor. It's the old story, Miss Florence. Printer's ink is a fluid possessing a fiendish charm. Who sees himself in print once is a slave of the dev — the printer's devil — forever.

Flos. (*crosses to* R.). Things will be duller than ever, I'm afraid. And now that you've found what you came to look for, you are going, too.

Cor. With a heavy heart.

Flos. (*innocently*). Then it isn't what you expected?

Cor. What?

Flos. What you were searching for.

Cor. No. It's extremely deceptive. At first it appeared to be really charming; but on examining it carefully and critically, I found it full of hidden defects.

Flos. Then you won't buy it?

Cor. That's the nonsensical part of it. I'm afraid I

shall take the thing after all—for, candidly, I'm quite in love with it.

FLOS.   In spite of the defects? You'll regret it hereafter.

COR. (*crosses to* L.).   That's what I'm afraid of, too. For that reason I applied for advice to my mother,—who is most interested, next to myself, — and she rather seems to encourage me. (*Produces letter from pocket.*) Here's her letter. But even if she didn't, I'm so infatuated I should go on. (*Puts up letter.*) There's no reasoning with a man in love.   [FLOSSY *crosses to* L., *and laughs.* Don't laugh at me.

FLOS. (L.).   Well, I won't. But you actually talk about this bric-a-brac as if it were a woman you were in love with. Why do you look at me so strangely?

COR. (R.).   Did I? (*Aside.*) Is this innocence, or is she playing with me?

FLOS.   I didn't mean to offend. A cat may look at a king — that's the old saying.

COR.   Yes — and we have no recorded saying as to who may look at the queen.

FLOS. (*crossing to* R., *archly*).   Why, all the animal kingdom. That includes man.

COR.   Pardon me if I offended by my stare — but I thought I saw a resemblance —

FLOS.   A resemblance to what?

COR.   To a portrait I saw at the Academy this year.

FLOS. (R.).   Indeed! How interesting!

COR. (*aside*).   Not a muscle changes. What a little dissembler she is!

FLOS.   It's a mere coincidence, of course.

COR. (*aside*).   She fibs like a newspaper — and looks as innocent as a Christmas doll.

FLOS.   I'd like to see the picture.

COR.   You'd be disappointed, for the young lady has the most unbecoming head of hair I ever saw.

FLOS. Of course! The idea of black curls with such eyes and that complexion. (*Confused.*) Ahem!

COR. How did you know the lady in the picture had black curls?

FLOS. (*aside*). That *was* a mistake. (*Moves away.*)

COR. (L.). Don't be angry with me for having been so rude as to trap you.

FLOS. (*turns in pretended innocence*). Trap me? Why, what do you mean? You haven't trapped me.

COR. No? (*Incredulously.*)

FLOS. No. (*Crosses to* L.)

COR. (*with a smile*). Oh!

FLOS. I heard all about the picture from Signor Tamborini.

COR. (*amazed*). O—o—h!

FLOS. (*sweetly*). Y—e—e—s! (*Goes up, leaving* COR-LISS C., *nonplussed; then she returns, and in the same gracious tone.*) Didn't you know we had a call from Signor Tamborini? He has been commissioned by Lord Lawntennis to discover the original of that very portrait.

COR. (*long drawl*). O—o—h!

FLOS. Y—e—s. (*Turning a little away.*)

               [*READY* JESSIE, *to enter* R. C.

COR. (*aside*). The little fox! She got out of it wonderfully.

FLOS. (*Assumes an injured and indignant air, and is sailing out* R.). Good-morning!

COR. (L.). Miss Florence — one moment.

FLOS. You have wronged me, Mr. Corliss, with the most unjust suspicions.

       [*READY* BARGISS, *with four pens, and* MRS. BAR-
          GISS, *to enter* L. D.

COR. Let me assure you, on my honor, I never entertained, concerning your truth and candor, one unjust suspicion.

FLOS. (*sharply*, R.). What's that? Say it again.

COR. No. Let me say I am full of contrition.

FLOS. That's better, and I forgive you — and — and — good-morning. (*EXIT*, R. 1 D.)

COR. (*solus*). And I am in love with such an utterly unreliable, imperfect, deceiving piece of womankind, or girlkind, as that! The idea of a frank, honest fellow selecting a creature like this for his life companion! And yet I'll do it. I feel it coming. (*Taking out his mother's letter.*) The answer I shall send to this will be an announcement of my engagement — if she'll have me. [*EXIT*, R. C., *as*

JESSIE *rushes in* R. C.

JESSIE (*almost runs against him*). The Professor's come! The Professor's come! (*Knocks at door*, L.) The Professor's come, ma'am!

ENTER MRS. BARGISS, L. D.

The wagon's just driving up, ma'am.

[*READY* GASLEIGH, *to enter* R. C.

MRS. BARGISS. Very well, Jessie; run up and see that everything's right in the Professor's room.

JES. Yes'm. (*EXIT*, R. 1 D.)

ENTER BARGISS, L. D., *two pens behind his ears, one in his mouth, and one in his hand.*

BARGISS. It is too bad to be disturbed just at this moment. I felt I was just becoming inspired.

MRS. B. (R.). Yes, dear.

BAR. Hypatia, I believe this time I'm going to make a hit.

MRS. B. (R.). Don't strain yourself too much, Launcelot.

BAR. I must make up for lost time. Stop! (*Inspired.*) There's an idea. (*Takes out a notebook and writes.*) The fountain, choked for years, bursts into play and overflows its basin. (*Crosses to* R., *and commences to write.*) .

MRS. B. Oh, how proud and happy all this makes me! Sh! Here's the Professor — who is destined to be the Boswell to your Johnson.

JESSIE *shows in* GASLEIGH, *a shrewd and not over prosperous-looking party*, R. C.

His anxiety to know you proves it, and he's come all the way from New York to see you.

GASLEIGH (C.). Madam, permit me to express my gratefulness at being permitted the opportunity of visiting genius in its own dwelling. (*He presses her outstretched hand.*)

MRS. B. (*effusively*, L.). Professor, you are welcome — allow me —

GAS. (*sees* BARGISS, *and takes an attitude*). Don't speak. That is Launcelot Bargiss — author of the "Pansy Chain." (*Crosses to* BARGISS *and takes both his hands.*) Let me take you by the hand. Let me salute the man who has stepped to his place in the ranks of literature at a single bound.

BAR. (R.). I'm glad to see you, Professor — very glad.

GAS. (*still holding his hands*). Yes — you are as I pictured you to myself. Half poet — half philosopher. All sensibility — generosity — capability — and hospitality. (*Taking his hand. To* MRS. BARGISS.) Do you know what I said to myself when I first read your husband's poems?

MRS. B. I should like very much to know, Professor.

GAS. I said, these verses are not written by some mere gushing youth. There is a man's heart throbbing beneath them.

MRS. B. Isn't there! Pray be seated.   [*All sit.*

BAR. But you know I was quite a boy when I wrote them.

GAS. I saw *that* in a moment. The effusions of youth —

but not *mere youth* — a man's heart *was* throbbing within them ! Mark the distinction.

BAR. I see.

MRS. B. That's why it vexed me so when the other publishers refused them.

GAS. Bless you! I understand all that. You were rejected because you weren't in the literary ring. It was that kind of thing induced me to start my periodical. The " Scattered Leaflets " have been founded as a refuge for the outcasts of the pen. In its pages such talent as yours challenges the public notice. We shall not longer allow Tennyson, Whittier, and Longfellow to monopolize celebrity.

BAR. Do you know, Professor, that, after the first gasp of pleasure at seeing my lines in print, I began to think as though —

GAS. I know — I know — you felt the power to soar higher, and disdained the flight already taken.

BAR. I didn't feel exactly like that. No — I thought the whole lot trash.

GAS. (C.; *all rise*). I comprehend. I know the feeling. Self-doubt is the true test of genius.

BAR. (R.). Is it? So you think there is something in 'em, eh? Well, I sha'n't confine myself to poetry ; it's too exhausting. (*Getting* C., *crosses*.)

GAS. No, no.

BAR. Yes. The rhymes don't come as they used to, and the measure has a sort of rheumatic limp.

GAS. (*aside*). Hum !

BAR. I've been thinking of the drama. The stage needs elevating.

MRS. B. It does, indeed.

BAR. I mean to check, as far as lies in my power, the degenerating influences now at work.

MRS. B. That will be splendid, Launcelot.

BAR. I've nearly finished a five-act tragedy. Which of the theatres would you advise me to send it to ?

GAS. Which of 'em? None of 'em. A few authors mo-nopolize the managers and keep all the new talent in the background.

MRS. B. That's true.

GAS. Do you know how the managerial ring works the little game of stifling competition? (*Crosses to* C.) They've got it down to a fine point. To have a play produced, you must have a name. To have a name, you must have your play produced. Ha, ha, ha! Do you see?

MRS. B. (L.). It's monstrous!

GAS. I'll change all that. The public shall see your play. Give it to me. I'll publish an act a month.

BAR. (*rises*). If you like I'll read it to you at once.

GAS. There'll be time enough after dinner.

BAR. (*crosses to* L.). Oh, we'll be able to get through a couple of acts before dinner. I'll run and get the manu-script from the library.

GAS. (*crosses to* C.). Very well. (*Produces a huge wallet and takes out a paper.*) And, if you don't mind, you can take the contract with you and sign at your leisure.

BAR. The contract? (*Takes it.*)

MRS. B. (R.). O Professor! Mr. Bargiss would not accept pay for his writings.

GAS. Ha, ha, ha! A slight mistake. It's a contract in which he subscribes for a dozen copies of the magazine. You see, what with the paper and the type-setting and the print-ing, expenses run up — run away up.

BAR. But, as a contributor, I thought —

GAS. Precisely — as a contributor, it's your interest to con-tribute to the support of the magazine.

BAR. But it seems to me that twelve at the start —

MRS. B. I rather expected we should get a free copy.

GAS. So you will — the thirteenth — that's our rule.

MRS. B. (R.). Oh, in that case it's quite satisfactory.

BAR. Yes, in that case I'll sign. Come along, Professor.

I'll read you those two acts. I've selected an historical subject. My tragedy is founded on an episode in the life of Charles the Fat.

GAS. Ha, ha, ha! (*Puts his hand on his stomach.*) Fat, eh? That puts me in mind of dinner. Ha, ha, ha!

[*EXIT* BARGISS, L., *shutting the door abruptly.* (*Aside.*) He doesn't take.

MRS. B. (*confidentially*). Now that we are alone for a moment, Professor, I have something important to arrange with you. I wish to give my husband the surprise of his life. When we were engaged to be married, he sent me every day a bouquet and two verses of poetry. We were engaged eight months.

GAS. Eight months? That makes two hundred and forty days. Two hundred and forty bouquets. Four hundred and eighty verses of poetry!

MRS. B. The flowers have long been withered, but the verses are carefully preserved in my desk. What I want is to have them published, with the utmost secrecy, in a volume.

GAS. I see.

MRS. B. Now, can you find me a publisher?

GAS. What do you want with a publisher? What makes the publishers rich? The profits they wring from the brain-toil of authors.

[*READY* HOLLYHOCK, *with hat, to enter* R. C.

MRS. B. What shall I do, then?

GAS. (L.). Publish them yourself. Strike the first blow at a gigantic monopoly — the publishers' ring. Your title-page will simply say : " Published by the author — written by the publisher." [*READY* MRS. HOLLYHOCK, *to enter* R. 3 D.

MRS. B. Can you attend to it for me?

GAS. (*grasps hands*). With pleasure.

MRS. B. I should like the binding to be extremely elegant.

GAS. I'll have a special design.

MRS. B. I'm so much obliged. But, mind, not a word to Mr. Bargiss.

GAS. Not a word. It's our secret.

MRS. B. It's the dream of my life. Launcelot's works elegantly bound, and lying on every parlor table in the land! I'll bring you the manuscript. (*EXIT,* R. I D.)

GAS. (*solus*). Now, these are the kind of people I like. But you have to look for 'em in the country. City people know too much! (*Looks around.*) I wonder when they have lunch. They don't seem to eat much. That's one drawback to literary people. But *I've* travelled four hours, and I'm as hungry as a bear. (*EXIT after* BARGISS, L. D.)

ENTER HOLLYHOCK, R. C.; *same costume as Act I. Throws down his hat and then goes back and speaks off.*

HOLLYHOCK. Tell him to wait. I'm busy just now. Wait a while.

ENTER MRS. HOLLYHOCK, R. 3 D.

MRS. H. Why, Paul, I thought you had to go to the mill.

HOL. (L.). Not before lunch. Hullo! What's the matter again? Now, you've been crying. (*Walks up and down.*)

MRS. H. I know I have. (*Crosses to* L.) I've been wanting to say something to you for a long time. Come here, Paul.

HOL. Oh, I can't now, Dora! I'm out of sorts, too. I want to know something myself, and my mind's full of it. Father could set me right, but since he's got this new fit on him, he neglects everything else. (*Still striding.*)

MRS. H. (*seated* L.). Oh, confide in me, Paul! Ask your wife. She is your true comforter. I have noticed that you act strangely of late — that you are preoccupied and sometimes even — indifferent.

Hol. My dear girl, there's a reason for it. It has begun to dawn on me that we must have a change.

Mrs. H. (*rises hopefully*). You see that yourself?

Hol. Yes; I've thought it all over, and I believe I've hit on the right thing.

Mrs. H. (l.). Really and truly?

Hol. Really and truly. What do you think— (*Walking away.*) But why should I bother you with my worries? (*Crosses to* c.)

Mrs. H. (*following him, and putting her arms lovingly about his neck*). Ah, confide in me, Paul.

Hol. (l.). Well, what do you think of the German system of feeding cows? They say the results are better for half the labor and quarter the money.

Mrs. H. Feeding cows!

Hol. They don't vary clover with corn and oats — their principle —   [Mrs. Hollyhock *goes away angrily.* Where are you going — what ails you?

Mrs. H. (*gets* r. *of table; bitterly*). I expected something far different.   [*READY* Corliss, *to enter* r. c.

Hol. Well, if you think the German system won't do, say so openly.

Mrs. H. Is this all you have to say to me?

Hol. Why, yes. Whole thing lies in a nutshell. It's grazing or stall-feeding — or varying the two. I don't see anything to object to in it.

Mrs. H. (*sitting, in tears*). You see nothing? O Paul!

Hol. (*going to her caressingly*). There is something wrong.

Mrs. H. (*rises, hand on his shoulder*). Can't you guess what is troubling me?

Hol. (*supporting her head on his shoulder*). Don't be afraid. Let me know everything. Is it — did you forget to moisten the pea-seed with the oil of turpentine?

Mrs. H. (*breaks away indignantly*). This is too much!

Hol. (*following*).   Dora!

Mrs. H. Let me alone! Oh! (*Bursts into tears, and EXIT* R. 3 D.)

ENTER Corliss, R. C.

Hol.   Dora!

Corliss (R.).   Pardon! I fear I have interrupted a domestic incident. (*Going.*)

Hol. (R.).   No, no.   Stay.   I can't tell you what came over my wife so suddenly. I tell you, Corliss, there isn't a husband in the land more uniformly considerate than I am, and yet latterly she seems to be always disturbed about something.

Cor. (L.).   You have unconsciously said something harsh.

Hol.   No, I didn't.   I didn't even blame her.   I mentioned the pea-seed and the oil of turpentine in the gentlest manner.

Cor. (*laughs*).   My dear friend, you are cultivating everything on this place to perfection — except your wife's happiness. Regaling a young wife upon turpentine and pea-seed! Why, man, it's love — love — love — and nothing but love she wants you to talk about.

Hol.   So I do occasionally — only last Wednesday —

Cor.   Last Wednesday!   Every day and every hour.

Hol.   Now, that I can't do.   There's really so much to look after about the place.   But when the potatoes are in —

Cor.   There you go.   Potatoes before your wife.   It's so the world over.   Molasses — sugar — corn — wheat — pig iron — books — stocks — bonds — everything before the wife! (*Crosses to* L.)

Hol.   But business before everything.

Cor.   It *is* business to make your wife happy.   The man who doesn't is a poor man of business, I don't care if he makes millions.

Hol. (R.).   Well, for a bachelor, you seem to have very profound views on the subject.   What do you advise?

COR.   I'm looking for advice myself (*takes out his mother's letter*) on the same subject.   Here is some of the very best from my mother, and yet I can't make up my mind.   (*Puts letter up.*)

HOL.   By the way — seeing your letter reminds me — I may have hurt my wife's feelings by some very stupid conduct.   You see, I noticed that she had some secret trouble; and a few days ago I thought I was on the track of it. She got a letter from New York which she refused to show me.

COR.   Oh!

HOL.   I afterwards found the envelope on the table there. Here it is.   (*Crosses to L. and hands envelope.*)

COR.   Well?   (*Takes it.*)

HOL.   Well, I questioned her so persistently about it that she finally hunted up the enclosure and gave it to me (*hands a paper*), and it was nothing but a milliner's circular.

COR.   What?   (*Takes it.*)

HOL.   Now, you see, she doubtless felt hurt at my questioning — I won't say suspicion in the matter, and that, with my neglect, perhaps —

COR.   Your diagnosis of the case is perfect.   She is suffering from a high degree of ennui, complicated by disappointment and distrust.

HOL.   And the remedy?

COR.   A winter in New York.

HOL. (L.).   A winter in New York!   I say, couldn't I give it to her in homœopathic doses — say a week now and then?

COR.   My dear fellow, nobody takes pleasure homœopathically.   She needs a change of air and scene, friends, visits, parties, theatres, balls, — everything she doesn't and can't get here.   (*Crosses to L.*)

HOL.   Well, but —

COR.   If you begin to butt against the remedy —

HOL. No, no. I'll have to think over it, though. I must look out for a furnished house.

COR. There's one just opposite my flat in the city. A new row near Central Park. Splendid view. Good air. No other neighbors. Quite a *rus-in-urbe*. You can hire it furnished for the season, and walk into it to-morrow.

[*READY* BARGISS, *with MSS., and* GASLEIGH, *to enter* L.

HOL. 'Gad, I'd start to-night if I made up my mind. I'm not so fond of dulness myself — only, if we live in the country, we must plod. If we live in town, we'll go it with the town. I'm afraid she mightn't like it as well as I should.

COR. Go and ask her. If she doesn't fly at your neck with a cry of joy, and fly at her trunks with a shout of victory — [*READY* MRS. BARGISS, *with MSS., to enter* R. 1 D.

HOL. (*crosses to* L., *interrupting him resolutely*). I'll try it instantly. (*Shakes his hand.*) Much obliged for the hint. I say — if you hear a cry of joy — telegraph at once for that house. (*EXIT,* R. 3 D.)

COR. (*fumbling the letter and envelope unconsciously*). It's wonderful how wise I am in other people's affairs, but when it comes to deciding for myself — (*In trying to put the circular into the envelope, he turns it different ways, but it won't fit, as the circular is long and the envelope is square.*) Hullo! This circular won't go into the envelope. Evidently because it never came out of it. My friend's wife has ventured a little deception on him. Possibly it's a quite harmless matter — but nevertheless, it's a trick. How fortunate he didn't discover it. I must warn her, however. (*Puts the circular and envelope in the same pocket with his mother's letter, and EXIT,* R. C.)

ENTER BARGISS, L., *followed by* GASLEIGH. BARGISS *with MSS.*

BARGISS. So, Professor, you like the play, eh? I'll mark

the place where we left off., Act 2d, scene 17th — and now we'll have luncheon.

GASLEIGH (L.). Don't speak of it. Your play was a feast for the gods.

[*READY* TAMBORINI *and* CORLISS, *to enter* R. C.

ENTER MRS. BARGISS, R. 1 D., *with bundle of MSS.*

MRS. BARGISS. Here it is. (*Hides her package as she sees* BARGISS.) Oh, my dear — would you mind leaving the Professor with me for a little while? I want to consult him.

BAR. (C.). Certainly, my love. I'll go and get a cracker and a glass of wine (*crosses to* L.) till lunch is ready. (*EXIT,* L.) [GASLEIGH *stretches out his hand, as if to detain him.*

GAS. I don't care if I do —

MRS. B. (*detains him*). Now, Professor, here are my treasures. I call them "Sonnets to a Fiancée." Wouldn't that make a capital title for our book?

GAS. (*exhibiting the cravings of hunger*). Capital.

MRS. B. I'll read you a few before lunch.

[GASLEIGH *groans.*

Come to my sitting-room. We won't be disturbed there.

GAS. But there's time enough. I'm in no hurry. You are perhaps too busy just now preparing for the meal.

MRS. B. Oh, not at all. We usually have a very light lunch. [GASLEIGH *groans..*

I'll begin now and finish in the afternoon. (*Going, reads a verse.*) Beautiful! Exquisite!

"Take — oh take those lips away
That so sweetly were forsworn."

[*EXIT,* R. 1 D.

GAS. I'm dying with hunger, and they fill me with wind.

[*EXIT,* R. 1 D.

ENTER TAMBORINI *and* CORLISS. R. C.

CORLISS (L.). So you find Lord Lawntennis is deeply interested in No. 728?

TAMBORINI (R.). *Si*, Signor. He's crazy. (*Gesture.*) Out of his head until he find the young lady who is the original.

COR. (*uneasy; aside*). The deuce! An English lord for a rival! This is likely to be very inconvenient.

TAM. I seek — but I find not.

COR. Then you have no clew to the young lady? (*Aside.*) Thank goodness! (*Crosses to* R.)

TAM. I knocked (*gesture*) at every door in the neighborhood where they send me. *Ma niente.* One haf no daughter. One haf seven (*counts them*), but they haf not been to Nahant. *Maledetto del' Ostia!* Another one haf a daughter, but she is so small. (*Gesture of baby in arms.*) Baby! Hush-a-by-rock-a-baby. *Corpo di bacco! Ma finalemente.* I found a young lady.

COR. The original?

TAM. *Non, ma dio!* There is a difference. The one is all gold on top — the other is *ebony.* But one, she is handsome. (*In ecstasy.*) *Sapette*, what shall I say! (*Searches for English in vain, and bursts into Italian.*) *Una bella ragazza con cecchi!* (*Points to eyes.*) *Cosi grandi!* (*Big eyes.*) *Una bocchina cosipiccola!* (*Small mouth.*)

COR. Yes, I know. Piccolo! (*Attitude of flute player.*)

TAM. *Ed ovechi* (*ears*)! *Ebbere una bellazza come non vide mai.*

COR. (*pats him on the back*). Very good, old fellow! My sentiments exactly. You describe her perfectly.

TAM. Ah! You laugh because you think my heart (*gesture*) run away (*gesture*) with my stupid head. (*Gesture.*)

COR. It all comes from your warm Italian blood — your sunny nature.

TAM. (L.). *Si, si.* The hot blood. In the American there is no heart — no pulse — but (*drowsily*) tick-a-tack, tick-a-tack (*marking time with his forefinger*). Ma, in my Italian veins, it is tick-a-tack, tick-a-tack! (*Very fast.*)

COR. Of course; we all know that. But what has brought you back to this house?

TAM. (*mysteriously*). It was — to make sure. There is a mystery.

COR. Indeed! (*Aside.*) Then he can't be got rid of too quickly. (*Stage, crosses to* L.)

TAM. (*cunningly*). I wish to study the young lady here once more.

COR. (*forgets himself*). The devil you do! (*Crosses to* L.; *turns back.*) You sha'n't do anything of the kind. (*Recovers.*) I mean, it will be a mere waste of time. The matter is quite simple. You were informed at Nahant that the young lady and her family *came* from this vicinity.

TAM. That is what they told me.

[*READY* FLOSSY, *to enter* R. C.

COR. You come here and you don't find her.

TAM. *Si, si.*

COR. That proves conclusively that you should have inquired not where she *came from* — but where she *went to.*

TAM. (*dilates with the idea of the thing*). I never thought of that.

COR. That's because in an Italian head the ideas go tick-a-tack, tick-a-tack (*imitates slowly*), while in the American cranium they go tick-a-tick, tick-a-tack. (*Very fast.*)

TAM. Ha, ha, ha! *Evero — E — vero!* That is good.

COR. So you must go at once to Nahant and begin again.

TAM. Of course! Of course!

COR. I recommend the greatest haste. A trail may be lost in a day. It's half-past twelve. (*Looks at watch.*) There's a train at 12.50.

TAM. I will just take leave of the Signora. They have been very kind.

Cor. You'll miss the express. Here, get your hat on (*opens it for him and puts it on*), and go at once. I'll give any message you choose to leave.

ENTER Flossy, r. c.

Flossy. Why, Signor, are you back again?

Cor. (*aside*). Too late!

Tam. Signorina! (*Profound bow, and aside to* Corliss.) The likeness is wonderful.

Cor. (*crosses to* c.). I beg you won't detain the Signor, Miss Florence. He has to start for Nahant at once.

Tam. But I —

Cor. (*seizes* Tamborini *by the lapel of the coat and pulls him round table towards* c.). The train is 12.50. You are losing time.

Flos. (*sweetly*). If you are going back to Nahant —

Cor. Yes — by the express.

Flos. (r.). Still seeking the original and unattainable?

Tam. *Si*, Signorina. Ah! If you would help me.

Flos. (r.). Is his lordship so impatient?

Cor. (l., *crosses to her suddenly*). I beg your pardon.

Flos. What is it?

Cor. You are losing the pin out of your hair. I'm afraid it's all coming down. (*Takes it out suddenly and hands it to her.*) It was just falling out.

Flos. (*claps one hand to her back hair and holds it. Takes the pin with the other*). Thank you — excuse me — only a minute. (*Runs out* r.)

Cor. (*sees her to the door*). All's fair in love. (*Stands with his back to the door — to* Tamborini.) You are saved. Fly to the station. You'll iust have time to catch that train.

Tam. (l., *looks at his watch*). *Madonna!* I must hurry. *A rivederci*, Signor. (*Profound bow, and then to himself.*) I will telegraph to his lordship that I am on the scent at last.

Oh, I guess I know whatever is what. (*To* CORLISS.) *A rivederci*, Signor. *A rivederci*. (*EXIT*, R. C.)

COR. (*coming from door*). At last! It was a tight squeeze. She's dazzled by his lordship, that's clear.

> [*READY* HOLLYHOCK *and* MRS. HOLLYHOCK, *to enter* R. 3 D.

FLOS. (*re-enters and looks for* TAMBORINI). Is he gone?

COR. Yes. I couldn't keep him any longer.

FLOS. (R.). Keep him? I rather thought you were trying to force him away.

COR. I plead guilty — for I wished to speak with you alone. I have an important communication to make to you — in the strictest confidence.

FLOS. Thank you — no more secrets. (*Crosses to* L.)

COR. It is not mine — it's your sister's.

FLOS. My sister's?

COR. Her husband has been hunting for a letter which she refused to show him. At last she was pressed so closely that she pretended to produce it. It was a circular which does not fit the envelope. Your brother-in-law did not notice the fact, and gave me the paper and envelope — but if he should ask for them —

HOLLYHOCK (*outside, at* R. *door*). Come along and tell him yourself.

COR. Sh! He's coming. There, give them to your sister. (*Crosses to* L.) My duty is done.

> [*Dives into his pocket and gives her, in his haste, his mother's letter with the other, as*

HOLLYHOCK *and* MRS. HOLLYHOCK *ENTER*, R. 3 D.

HOLLYHOCK (R.). There, my love, is the man who put it in my head. Make your acknowledgments.

> [*READY* JOBBINS, *to enter* R. C.

MRS. HOLLYHOCK (*crosses — gives hand to* CORLISS). How nice of you. When you marry, your wife will have a splendid husband, I'm sure.

COR. (*crosses to* HOLLYHOCK). I don't know. He may turn out like the rest of 'em. Think more of his potatoes than of her.   [HOLLYHOCK *and* CORLISS *go up* R.

MRS. H. (L.). Just think, Flos—we are going to New York for the winter. The house is taken, and we start to-morrow.

FLOS. (L. C.). Sh! I have something particular to give you. Come one side where Paul can't see us.

> [*They go up and* FLOSSY *explains, holding the papers in her hand as she speaks.*

HOL. (*down* R.). I'm really thankful to you. (*Shaking hands with* CORLISS.) You should have seen how happy she was. She was speechless.

COR. That's fortunate — I mean that's likely — I mean that's all right.

HOL. I had no idea a woman could change so quickly. I suppose you were waiting to hear that cry of joy.

COR. (R. C.). Yes, I want to telegraph for the house. Well, it's settled. When do you start?

JOBBINS *appears*, R. C.

HOL. To-morrow. They'll get on without me here. I'll give Jobbins, our farmer, his instructions. Oh, there he is.

JOBBINS. One moment, if you please, Mr. Paul.

HOL. (*joining* JOBBINS). Jobbins, you're just the man I want to see.   [CORLISS *saunters up.*

MRS. H. (*to* FLOSSY). Heavens, what a mistake!

FLOS. (*handing the papers*). So here they are. Now I've done my duty. (*Crosses to* C. *and exchanges signs with* COR-LISS.)   [CORLISS *joins* HOLLYHOCK.

MRS. H. (L., *aside*). I must tell Paul the whole truth at once. After all, what great harm was there in Flos having her picture painted? (*Looks at papers in her hand, and sees* CORLISS's *letter*.) This isn't mine, Flossy!

FLOS. What?

MRS. H.   You gave me one of your letters in mistake. (*Gives the letter, and goes up to* HOLLYHOCK, R. C.)

FLOS.   One of mine?   (*Opens letter.*)   What is this?   My name!   (*Reads over rapidly — turning letter over to see signature and address.*)

HOL. (*at back*, R. C., *to* JOBBINS, *cheerfully*).   Just fix it any way you like.   And mind, Jobbins, don't send to ask me anything after I'm gone.   I won't answer, I warn you! (*Talks with* MRS. HOLLYHOCK *and* CORLISS.)

FLOS. (*aside, flaring up*).   This is too much!   It's a letter from his mother, and about me.   (*Reads and sits on sofa*, L.) "I think you mix up her graver faults with lighter ones, and estimate both at the same value.   Now, to me, the fact that she is coquettish, romantic, hot-headed, and fond of admiration, is more serious than the fact that she touches the wrong keys at her piano-lesson or spells vinegar with an e-r."   (*Crumples the letter.*)   It's maddening!

[*READY* MRS. BARGISS, *to enter* R. I D.

JOB.   Well, Mr. Bargiss won't take no interest —

HOL.   Oh, let the whole thing go, then.

JOB.   But, Mr. Paul —

HOL.   I tell you I won't be bothered any more.   I've given up farming.   (*Taking his wife around the waist, and down* L.)   I'm going to spoon a bit.

[*EXIT* JOBBINS, R. C.   HOLLYHOCK *and* MRS. HOL-
LYHOCK *up to window*, L. C.

FLOS.   So *I* was the *thing* he came here to inspect!   I'm the piece of tapestry — the bric-a-brac with the internal defects.   The man's impudence passes all bounds.   Oh! I could —

COR. (*unconscious, comes down to her*, R.).   I hope, Miss Florence, we shall have the pleasure of seeing you in the city this winter.

[*READY* BARGISS, *with sandwich, napkin, and
glass of wine, to enter* L. D.

FLOS. (*looks at him; then bitingly*). Excuse me (*crosses to* R.), Mr. Corliss. I have something to do in my room. I must practise at my piano a couple of hours, and take another lesson in spelling vinegar. Good-morning! (*Bounces out*, R. I D.)

COR. (*astonished*). What's wrong now? That's a new phase of her character — sudden squalls. She's wonderful.

ENTER MRS. BARGISS, R. I D., *speaking off.*

MRS. BARGISS. No. G-a-r. Now, don't hurry. Finish your sherry and read the rest.

MRS. H. (*crosses to* C., *releasing herself from* HOLLYHOCK). Here's mamma.

MRS. B. Ah, there you are. I want your assistance. Your father must be persuaded to go to New York; if not permanently, at least for a season.

MRS. H. (*going to sofa*, L.). We are with you, mamma.

MRS. B. (*to* CORLISS, R. C.). I count on you, too, Mr. Corliss. (*To* MRS. HOLLYHOCK.) Where's your father?

MRS. H. In his room, I think.

MRS. B. (*crosses to* L. C.). He's killing himself. He's tying himself down so close to his literary labors down here, Mr. Corliss, that I'm sure he'll kill himself. (*Goes to door* L., *and knocks.*) Are you busy, darling? Can you leave off for a moment and come out?

BARGISS (*outside* L. D.). I can come out, but I can't leave off, Hypatia.

ENTER BARGISS, *eating a sandwich and drinking from a glass of sherry — napkin under his chin.*

What is it, darling?

MRS. B. Oh, I'm so glad to see you eat. (*To others.*) He never eats down here. (*To* BARGISS.) Professor Gasleigh has made a most valuable suggestion. If you act on it, you secure the success of your literary career.

BAR. (*eating*). No! What is it?

MRS. B. All life and movement is in the city—in New York. We can accomplish nothing in this out-of-the-way place. We must be on the spot.

> [*READY* GASLEIGH, *with sandwich, wine, and hand-kerchief, to enter* R. 1 E.

BAR. Does the Professor advise that?

MRS. B. Certainly. If you work for the public, you must live in public. If you wish people to know you, you must know people. Am I not right, Mr. Corliss?

COR. It's quite conclusive.

HOL. (L.). Come with us, father-in-law. We start to-morrow.

BAR. You do?

MRS. H. (*crossing to* HOLLYHOCK). Yes, papa.

MRS. B. You see the children even understand what's good for them.

> [*READY* JESSIE *and* FLOSSY, *to enter* R. C. *and* R. 1 D.

HOL. We do. (*Attempts to clasp* MRS. HOLLYHOCK. *She eludes him under her mother's eye.*)

BAR. Well, I'm willing. There's no need for much pressure. In fact, I had the same idea myself.

HOL. *and* MRS. H. Bravo, papa!

MRS. B. (*hurries to door,* R.). Come in, Professor. We've succeeded. Come in.

ENTER GASLEIGH, R. 1 E., *with a sandwich and sherry. Handkerchief tucked under his chin. He and* BARGISS *meet* C. *Both eat and drink simultaneously à la Dromios.*

GASLEIGH. I congratulate you. This is a great moment. If Guttenberg, when he invented the art of printing, could have foreseen a triumph like this, he would— (*His eye meets* CORLISS'S, *who stands up* R. *smiling calmly at the group, and he stops.*) Ah—another son-in-law of yours, Mr. Bargiss?

BAR. (*crosses to* CORLISS). No, sir—this is a young friend, a theorist, who says that every man in the world is bound to make a great ass of himself once in his life; aims too high and boomerangs himself.

GAS. (C.). We defy him and his theory.

ENTER JESSIE, R. C.

JESSIE. Luncheon is ready.

ENTER FLOSSY, R. I D.

[*READY curtain.*

FLOSSY. Here I am, papa.

BAR. (*to* GASLEIGH). Give your arm to Mrs. Bargiss.

[GASLEIGH *crosses to* MRS. BARGISS.

Mr. Corliss, give your arm to Flos.

[CORLISS *crosses to* FLOSSY.

FLOS. (*crosses to* BARGISS, *passing* CORLISS). No, papa; I'll take you. (*Takes* BARGISS's *arm as he faces up.*)

BAR. Ha, ha, ha! Sorry for you, Corliss. This comes of boomerangs. (*As all go off.*)

COR. We shall see. (*Goes up with* HOLLYHOCK *and* MRS. HOLLYHOCK.) [*RING curtain.*

CURTAIN.

ACT III.

SCENE. — An elegant apartment in a New York flat. To the window, L. 1 E., there is a practicable ledge or shelf and a shade. Also heavy curtains. The door to the room down stage R., opens out. There is a tall mirror, R., between the doors. Near window, L., a desk covered with writing-materials. A revolving book-holder beside it. Bust of Dickens and two candelabra on desk. On mantel-shelf, C., a bust of Shakespeare and two candelabra. Divan, C. Table and easy-chairs in front of chimney, C. Doors, R. C.; R. 1 E.; R. 3 E.; and L. 3 E. Door opening into second room, L. C. Chandelier, C.

"Nature" *Waltz from* "The Merry War," *at rise of curtain. Begin before curtain.* JESSIE *discovered, arranging flower in her hair before the mirror.* READY TAMBORINI, *to enter* L. C.

JESSIE (*waltzing*).

"Fair Melanie — so they say all can see,
  Loved fair nature, only nature,
  As she roamed the wild wood free ;
  Oh, what delight fills the heart, heaves the breast,
  When all dreaming, idly dreaming, 'neath the trees one lies to rest."

(*Speaks.*) Oh, how that music do go through me. I can never raise my arms to do a bit of work when I hear a waltz nowadays, and I've been to three balls in three weeks — and another one to-night, if I can get off to go. I'm going to wear Missis' garnet silk. She so seldom wears it. It

can't make no matter to her whether it stays packed away
in her trunk, or whether it goes to the ball with me. And
I've sewed on a pair of Mrs. Bargiss's mousquetaire tops to
my three-buttoned kids. The bracelets will just cover the
seams. Oh, that music! (*Sings and waltzes.*) Oh! I do
hope they'll play that waltz to-night. I got these flowers
from Miss Florence's old leghorn. They'll make a lovely
wreath. Oh, I wouldn't miss the ball to-night for a million.
(*Gets up stage,* R.; *comes down with waltz step, and waving her
arms.*)

ENTER TAMBORINI, L. C.; *he is entranced by the music, and
dances ad lib. At the finish she is about to fall, and he
catches her à la ballet, holding his opera-hat over her head.*

Why — Mr. Tamborini! (*Runs down with a little cry.*)
             [*READY* MRS. BARGISS, *to enter* R. 1 D.

TAMBORINI (R.). It was beautiful. It was *exquise*.
Brava! Brava! Ah, you make a *prima ballerina*, my child.
You have the *applomb*, the *abandon*, the throw of the true
ballet.

JES. Do you think so, Mr. Tamborini? I do so love
music and dancing.

TAM. *Basta!* There is no music any more. This Keelperd and Zolifon style of thing is all stuff.

JES. (L.). Keelperd? Oh, you mean Gilbert and Sullivan.

TAM. And there is no more ballet in this country. In-
stead of talking-with the eye, the hand, the finger, the foot,
the toe — they come down to talk with the poor little insig-
nificant tongue that nobody can see. (*Enthuses.*) Ah! Ah!
If you come with me to my country, I show you some things.

JES. (*coolly waves him off*). Yes. Exactly. But please
— who do you wish to see — old Missis or young Missis?
             [*He makes an enthusiastic dash for her.*
(*She bobs under his arm and bounds off* R.) I'll go and tell
them both you're here. (*EXIT,* R. 1 E.)

TAM. (*kissing his hand after her*). *Una bella!* The Signora Bargiss have send for me! A mysterious communication that she can give me perhaps some information about the portrait.

ENTER MRS. BARGISS, R. I D., *preceded by* JESSIE.

JESSIE. Missis is coming.

MRS. BARGISS. Oh, have you come, Signor?

[*READY* CORLISS, *to enter* L. C.

TAM. Signora! (*Profound bow.*) I have received your little letter.

MRS. B. (*to* JESSIE). Tell Miss Florence I wish to see her. [JESSIE *goes off,* R. C., *attitudinizing till off.* (*To* TAMBORINI.) Have you been to Nahant?

TAM. *Si*, Signora, by the express train. (*Gesture.*) I found nothing but the cold weather that freeze — the ice, the snow, and the hotels shut up like everybody was dead.

MRS. B. (R.). I wrote you that I might be able to give you a hint regarding the original of that portrait.

TAM. (*ecstasy*). Ah, Signora, if I could only telegraph the smallest gleam of hope to his lordship!

MRS. B. Possibly you may. I cannot announce anything definite as yet — but I have a few important questions to ask you first about his lordship.

TAM. Signora! Ask me everything. Here is my whole heart. (*As if tearing it out and offering it with both hands.*) Make your own selection. What do you want to know?

MRS. B. Come into the library. We shall be undisturbed.

TAM. *Ma si* — with pleasure. (*Follows her, keeping step to dance music, which still continues. She turns. He checks himself and bows profoundly.*) *La piego*, Signora, *la piego*.

[*EXEUNT*, R. I D.

ENTER JESSIE, R. C., *with a pair of* FLOSSY'S *shoes.*

JESSIE. Yes, Miss Flos. I'll see to it.

ENTER Corliss, L. C.

Corliss. Will you have the kindness to give my card to Miss Florence at once? Ah, Jessie! Wasn't Signor Tamborini here just now?

Jes. (*laughs*). Yes, sir. I should think he was.

Cor. What did he want? [*READY* Flossy, *to enter* R. C.

Jes. I don't know. He's with Mrs. Bargiss now in the library. (*Crosses to* L.) But he danced for me most beautiful, and tra-la-la'd divinely. (*Imitates* Tamborini, *holding the slippers over her head in her L. hand.*)

Cor. (R.). What are those?

Jes. Miss Flossy's shoes.

Cor. (*aside*). Charming slippers! (*To* Jessie.) And you are sure Signor Tamborini didn't see her?

Jes. Oh, sure.

Cor. (*gives her money*). Add that to your collection of coins. (*Stroking the slippers.*) Dear little slippers!

Jes. (*laughs*). He, he, he! (*Going.*) Oh, he *is* in love! I'm so glad! (*EXIT*, L. C.)

Cor. She laughs at me. She's right. I am a fair subject for ridicule. I'm growing more and more in love with this girl every day, and yet I don't know whether she cares a rap for me or not. Haven't been able to bring her to an explanation since she's been in New York. All I do is to stand at my windows opposite and gaze at these windows. She never appears. And now this infernal Italian is back again. I must get the start of him, and have an understanding with Flos at once.

ENTER Flossy, R. C. *Home evening dress.*

Flossy. O Mr. Corliss! (*Going down* R.)

Cor. Won't you grant me a short interview?

Flos. I would with pleasure, but mamma has sent for me.

Cor. I should feel greatly obliged if you would give me

the preference, as I have been watching my opportunity for some days.

FLOS. (*aside*). And so have I.

COR. I have something to say which I could not utter to any other ear on earth but yours.

FLOS. That's very odd. Won't you be seated? (*Aside.*) Now he'll find out whether he can get the bric-a-brac he's looking for, or not. If I died the next minute, I'd say no. (*Sits* R.)

COR. (*seated* C.). May I speak candidly?

FLOS. You can do your best. *I* hate all subterfuges.

COR. Then, Miss Florence — in one short word —

FLOS. (*interrupting purposely*). *Apropos*, did you know that Signor Tamborini has returned?

COR. (*indifferently*). Indeed! (*Aside.*) I wish I had sent him to Russia.

FLOS. Are you acquainted with Lord Lawntennis?

COR. I never met his *lordship*. His reputation abroad, I believe, is that of a crack-brained sportsman. He came here to hunt buffaloes. History is silent as to any other particulars. But to return to our subject. What I have to say may —

FLOS. (*as before*). Pardon me — another question. Can you tell me — as an authority on such matters — they say you know everything — how the wife of an English earl ranks at the European courts — especially at Berlin and St. Petersburg?

COR. Does his lordship interest you so much?

FLOS. Isn't it quite natural? The story sounds like a fairy-tale; so unlike our matter-of-fact customs. A noble earl falls in love with the portrait of a girl — with her portrait only — without knowing anything about her — without caring for anything except that he loves her (*significantly*) — and not even asking who she is — what she is — sends his messenger to find her and —

Cor.   And lay his hand and title at her feet.   You think she ought to feel very happy?

Flos.   To be the wife of a millionaire lord — unquestionably.

Cor.   And yet she knows nothing of him except that his name and his fortune are real.   That is very little.

Flos.   And, pray, what is wanting?

Cor.   The one thing without which there can be no happiness.   Let me quote from Heine, —

> " Angels call it Heavenly bliss,
> The demons call it Hell's abyss,
> But mortals call it Love."

Flos. (*laughs*).   Ha, ha, ha!   Oh, love!   (*Crosses to* L.) Ha, ha, ha!   Love, to be sure!   Excuse me for laughing. I know nothing about it, although the novels I've read are quite full of the subject, and very charming it is *there*.   But what little I've seen in real life appears to me utterly unreliable.

Cor. (*rises*).   Why, Miss Florence?

Flos. (*sarcastically*).   Because the gentlemen of to-day appear to set too high a value on their love and too little on ours.   They think it sufficient to come grandly forward, after a severe internal struggle at giving up their freedom, and say to the girl: "I love you."   It's this overpowering sense of their giving everything and getting nothing — this doing a favor and making a sacrifice and driving a bargain, that repels and exasperates me.   I don't call that love.   (*Crosses to* R., *changing her tone and position suddenly.*)   But you had something to say to me.   (*Sits* R. C.)

Cor. (*hesitating*).   Had — had I?

Flos. (*impatiently*).   Didn't you ask me for an interview?

Cor. (*sits* c.; *low tone*).   Yes.   But that's all over now.   I — I have nothing to say.

[*READY* Mrs. Bargiss, *to enter* R. 1 D.

FLOS. (*rises*).   Indeed!   Then I may consider myself dismissed?·

COR. (*making a step*).   I beg of you —

FLOS.   Pray, make no excuses.   If you are not as polite as usual, the fault is doubtless mine.   It sha'n't happen again. (*Going to door,* R.)

COR. (*hotly*).   You shall not leave me like that.   You *shall* listen to me.

[*READY* JESSIE, *with candelabrum, letters, and pa·pers, to enter* L. C.

FLOS. (*with varying feeling*).   Oh, no, I shall not.   I will not listen to you now — nor hereafter.   Excuse my departure. Good-evening. (*EXIT,* R. I D., *hiding her own emotion.*)

COR. (*solus*).   That was plain enough.   But what could I expect?   She's dazzled by a title and wealth like all the rest. Merely human and natural. (*Suddenly.*)   No, it's not.   To look like an angel — beguile a poor wretch, and then cut him off with questions about earls' wives and court etiquette — and yet I feel I could win her.   I know how, if I could only do it — if it wasn't so impossible for a man in love to preserve his common-sense.

ENTER MRS. BARGISS, R. I D.

MRS. BARGISS.   I heard you had called, Mr. Corliss.

COR.   I won't keep you — from your visitor.

MRS. B.   Signor Tamborini?   Oh, he's going.   I left Flos to see him off.   Pray, stay a minute longer.   I haven't had an opportunity of telling you how greatly we are indebted to you for getting us this house.

[*READY* BARGISS, *with four pens, to enter* L. D.

COR. (L.).   I trust your visit to the city fulfils your expectations.

MRS. B.   To be honest — not quite.

ENTER JESSIE, L. C.; *she brings in a candelabrum, not lighted, and some letters and papers.   Puts former on table near mantel, and arranges papers on desk near window,* L.

COR.   Indeed?

MRS. B.   It will prove of great value to my husband's literary future, of course (*he bows*); but as for me, I'm not used
to being left so much alone.   Paul and Dora have found their
city friends, and are never at home.   My husband is away all
day with the Professor, and spends his nights writing in his
study.

COR.   I have noticed, from my window opposite (*points*),
that he keeps his lamp burning until daylight.   (*Gets* L.)

JESSIE. (*at desk*, L.; *turns suddenly to* MRS. BARGISS *with a
cry*).   Oh, dear!   Oh, ma'am!   That reminds me — Mr. Bargiss's lamp.

MRS. B.   Well, what's the matter with Mr. Bargiss's lamp?

JES.   I took it to be mended yesterday morning, and forgot to bring it back.   I'll go for it at once.   (*EXIT*, L. C.)

MRS. B.   Then he had no lamp last night.   That accounts
for his being put out all this morning.   He didn't mention it,
but I knew something was wrong.   '(*Crossing to desk*, L.)

ENTER BARGISS, L. D., *pens behind his ears, one in his mouth.
and one in his hand, as before.*

BARGISS.   Has the mail come, Hypatia?   Ah, how are you,
Corliss?

MRS. B. (*gets letters, etc., from desk, and gives them to him*).
Here it is, dear.   You look worried, darling.   I'm so sorry
you are vexed.

BAR. (*opening paper*).   It's only natural — sitting up all
night to write.   I'm simply overworked, Hypatia.

MRS. B.   But you were not writing last night, surely.

BAR. (*yawning, and looking through paper*).   Ye — es.   I
was busy at my society novel.

[MRS. BARGISS *looks at him and then at* CORLISS.
(BARGISS *goes on lying, unconscious of their glances.*)   It's a
strange thing now, Mr. Corliss — but I can work only at

night. When every one is in bed — when all the rest of the world sleeps — I go on, adding chapter to chapter.

COR. (R. C., *trying to help him out*). Oh, yes — I see — by the light of your solitary candle — like Tasso in his dungeon. (*He makes signs to* BARGISS, *who fails to take.*)

BAR. Candle? No, I always work with a lamp.

MRS. B. (L.). Launcelot, did you work last night with a lamp, too?

BAR. Certainly, my love — why not? (L. C., *crosses to* R.)

MRS. B. (*recoiling, sotto voce,* L.). And there was no lamp there! (*Aloud.*) Launcelot!

COR. (*takes his hat — aside.*) The lamp is about to explode. I'll get out of the way. [*EXIT,* L. C.

MRS. B. Launcelot!

BAR. (R. *walks up*). Now what's the matter with you?

MRS. B. Your lamp has been gone for repairs the last two days.

BAR. (*appalled, his jaw falls; a moment's pause. Sinks in chair* R. *of divan.*) Heavens!

[*READY* GASLEIGH, *to enter* L. C.

MRS. B. You have told me a falsehood, Launcelot — a petty, mean falsehood — a falsehood to cover some hidden wickedness. Oh! (*Sinks on divan,* C.)

BAR. (*starting up*). My dear, let me explain.

MRS. B. Explain! (*Rises.*) I should think so. You shall explain where you have been passing your nights — for this isn't the first time, I'm sure of it.

BAR. (R. C.). First and foremost, my dear, Professor Gasleigh —

MRS. B. Never mind Professor Gasleigh. You have been guilty of a shameful deception. You've kept that lamp burning in your room every night — nobody dared to go in for fear of disturbing you. When I woke in the middle of the night, I sighed to think how you were toiling — and you were not there — you — (*In awful tone.*) Where were you, Launcelot?

BAR. (*rises*, R.). I was out with Gasleigh. [*She groans.* (*He echoes her groan.*) Just listen to me, and don't growl in that infernal manner.

MRS. B. I won't listen. I know the worst is coming.

GASLEIGH *appears at* L. C.

GASLEIGH. May I come in? (C.) Are we resting from our toil, eh? What chapter have we got to? Have we reached the climax, eh?

BAR. (R.). Yes, I guess we have.

MRS. B. You come in very good time, sir. I shall be glad to hear your version of this scandalous affair.

BAR. My wife won't believe —

MRS. B. How can I ever again believe what you tell me?

GAS. (*aside to* BARGISS). What is it?

BAR. (*aside*). My lamp was at the shop getting repaired last night.   [GASLEIGH *whistles.*

MRS. B. Is this the customary thing among you literary men?

GAS. (*aside to* BARGISS). She knows you were out?

BAR. (*same*). Every night. Fix it up. Fix it up. (*Nudges* GASLEIGH. MRS. BARGISS *almost detects him, as she crosses* C. *He pretends to be smoothing something in his sleeve.*)

MRS. B. (C.). Where have you and my husband been?

GAS. (L., *boldly*). At work.

MRS. B. (*to* GASLEIGH). At work?

BAR. At wo—   [MRS. BARGISS *turns and looks at him.* —ork.

MRS. B. By lamplight?

GAS. No, my dear madam. Do you think a poet labors only at his desk? This is the least and the last of his toil. He must go forth — mingle with his kind — and study every phase of human nature.

MRS. B. Is it necessary to do that at night?

GAS. The nature of man is furtive, like the savage beast.

At night it emerges from its den and prowls. We have tracked it to its lair. I may incidentally mention that we have gone where, if we were not poets, we could not have ventured with propriety.

MRS. B. (*shocked*). Launcelot!

GAS. (L.). Our mission preserved us from contamination. Your husband is writing a novel of life — how can he picture vice unless he sees it?

BAR. You hear, my dear?

GAS. The dark side of life is invisible by day. Look at Dickens —

BAR. Yes, my dear — look at Dickens — Charley.

GAS. He wandered through the slums of London in disguise.

BAR. Never came home for days.

GAS. Do you think he asked his wife's permission to make that pilgrimage of duty?

BAR. Certainly not.

MRS. B. (C.). But your health, Launcelot. You can't stand it. You are not strong.

BAR. Oh, yes I am. I'm bound to the wheel. What matters it? The spirit may burst its bounds. Let it come.

MRS. B. But why not have told me? Why deceive your own wife? I could have seen that you were comfortably wrapped up before you went out.

GAS. Poets love mystery, my dear madam.

BAR. (R., *taking her hand affectionately*). I wanted to spare you anxiety, my darling.

GAS. That was his only solicitude.

BAR. (R., *brings* MRS. BARGISS *down*). You see, it's all right.

MRS. B. (*sighs*). I don't know.

BAR. I didn't do it for the sake of pleasure. Many a time, in a scene of gayety, I've wished myself somewhere else,   [*She presses his hand.* so we went somewhere else. (*Crosses to* C.)

[*She looks at him dubiously.*
But I've collected enough material for my society novel,
and now, thank goodness, I can stay at home.

Mrs. B. O Launcelot, if you only —

Bar. (L. *of* Mrs. Bargiss). Let's say no more about it.
Go and wash your eyes, so the children won't notice anything. There — there —

Mrs. B. (*aside, going*). I begin to think it would have
been better if we hadn't come to this wicked city. (*EXIT,
R. 1 D.*)

Bar. (*to* Gasleigh). Got out of it better than I could
have expected. It's a shame to impose upon her. A better
woman never lived.

Gas. Lucky for you. I wish I could get out of my
trouble so easily.

Bar. What's the matter?

Gas. My printer refuses to go on without money. The
" Scattered Leaflets " must stop. Just when the circulation
was increasing, too. Your new poem was to come out in the
next number. It would have made a tremendous sensation.

Bar. What's to be done?

Gas. Pay or stop. (*Stage* R.)

Bar. How much does he want?

Gas. (*sinks on chair*, R. C.). No matter. Let it go. But
I should like to have had the credit of bringing out that
poem of yours. Still, none of us can accomplish all we
dream of. Let it go.

Bar. (L.). Don't be down-hearted, old fellow. Tell me
how much it is.

Gas. A trifle. A mere bagatelle. A beggarly, pitiful
trifle. One of the grains of sand that genius stumbles over
and breaks its neck. A mean, pitiful, little, petty three hundred dollars.

Bar. Three hundred dollars!! I'll give you a check for
it. There — cheer up.

GAS. (*rises — firmly*). No, no ; you shall not.

BAR. Yes, I will.

GAS. Never ! Let it perish. Let me perish. Let the magazine perish.

BAR. No, no. I don't care for my own part, but it gives my wife so much pleasure to see me in print, that I'll pay any reasonable sum to gratify her.

GAS. (*seizes his hand*). Bargiss, you are a great man. Bargiss, there's more poetry and fact in that speech than in all Byron's works bound together.

BAR. (*cheerfully*). My forte may be poetry. I'm pretty sure it isn't prose. My novel doesn't seem to get on. Collecting material is quite jolly — but I don't see my way to piecing the thing out. By the way — talking of piecing — how's my piece getting on ? Have you seen the managers ?

GAS. (R.). You can't see the managers. They are never in. I've sent Charles the Fat to them all — and he's back on our hands.

BAR. Must have lost some flesh in going the round, eh ?

GAS. We'll carry out my first idea, and print it act by act in the " Scattered Leaflets." Then you'll have the whole crowd begging for it. Now, they won't even read it.

BAR. (L.). Won't read it ? Won't read the new plays sent them ? What on earth have they got to do ?

GAS. By the way, you spoke of your want of practical experience in theatrical matters, and wanted to go —

BAR. (*quickly*). Behind the scenes.

GAS. (*triumphantly*). We can get on the Academy stage to-night in the auxiliary corps — how's that ?

BAR. As supernumeraries, eh ? What's the opera ?

    [*READY* HOLLYHOCK *and* MRS. HOLLYHOCK, *in full dress, with wraps, to enter* L. C.

GAS. I don't know; but you go as a high priest.

BAR. Ain't I rather short for a high priest ?

GAS. A tall hat and a long beard make you all right. Then you'll have a first-rate chance to study the whole mechanism of the stage — scenery — decorations — actors — and dancers. (*Dig in side.*)

BAR. No! I really think it indispensable, don't you?

GAS. There's only or.: difficulty — your wife. Will she consent, or must you slip off?

BAR. (*decisively*). We'll slip off this time. Just once more — then we'll shut down. (*Crosses to* R.)

GAS. How will you manage? The lamp no longer holds out to burn.

BAR. (*struck with an idea*). Stop — I can have a head-ache — and then go to the study and lie down — lock my-self in so as to be undisturbed. You engage her in conver-sation, then I vanish.

> [*Mutual crossing and turn up stage. Take hands as they advance, singing from* " Puritani."

(*Suddenly stops and puts his hand on* GASLEIGH'S *mouth.*) Sh! Here come the children. (*Crosses to* L.) I'll go and make out that check for you. (*EXIT, followed by* GAS-LEIGH, L. D.)

ENTER HOLLYHOCK *and* MRS. HOLLYHOCK, L. C., *in full dress and with wraps, as if from street. Both very gay and fashionable. They take off over-wraps as they talk.*

MRS. HOLLYHOCK (R.). Thank goodness, we are home again. I'm ready to drop.

HOLLYHOCK. I feel as fresh as a daisy. Let me assist you.

MRS. H. Oh! (*Sinks on divan,* C.) Fresh as a daisy, in-deed? That dinner has just ended me. We have been on the go from morning till night. Drive, park, lunch, *matinée,* receptions, Delmonico's — I want to go to bed. (*Yawns.*)

HOL. Lie down for an hour, darling, and you'll be ready for the theatre.

MRS. H. (*eyes closed*). Have we got to go to the theatre to-night?

    [*READY* BARGISS, *with bank-check, and* GASLEIGH, *to enter* L. D.

HOL. The Evartses asked us, you know. They have a box. I got a bill at the hotel to see what it was. (*Takes out a large handbill from his tail-pocket.*) It's Janauschek in two of her best parts, — tragedy and comedy. "Leah, the Forsaken," and "Come Here." Come here — that makes you want to go there, doesn't it? How's the attraction? (*Spreads it out over his chest.*)

MRS. H. (*languidly*). I don't feel like stirring.

HOL. Every woman ought to see "Come Here." It's an example for 'em. Nobody talks in the whole piece but the man. Awful warning to the sex. (*Lays bill on* C. *divan.*)

MRS. H. (*on divan*). Let's stay home for once.

HOL. (*dissatisfied*). We needn't have come to New York to do that. (*Crosses and sits* R.)

MRS. H. I hardly recognize you, Paul. Since we left home you have changed your whole nature. You can't rest —you burn for excitement.

HOL. The spirit of the metropolis, my darling. It's in the air.

MRS. H. But you overdo it, darling. Now, sit down calmly while I preach a sermon.

HOL. Heavens! (*Brings chair to her.*)

    [*She talks soothingly while he gesticulates forcibly.*

ENTER BARGISS, L. D., *with* GASLEIGH, *handing him a check.*

BARGISS. There you are. That will keep the "Scattered Leaflets" together for a while longer. (*They go aside,* L.)

HOL. (*to* MRS. HOLLYHOCK). Well, I'm content for to-night. But to-morrow we must go to the opera. Your mother asked Tamborini to get us a box. There's a rush to see the new contralto. (*Rises and comes forward briskly.*) I say, father-in-law, will you go with us? No, you can't. You're too busy.

BAR. (*suddenly putting his hand to his head*). I can't — I've got such a headache. Oh!

MRS. H. O papa! That's overwork. I know it's caused by what you've been doing. (*Stage* R.)

BAR. (*aside*). No, it's caused by what I'm going to do.

MRS. H. Can't you take a little rest?

BAR. (L., *crossing to* MRS. HOLLYHOCK). Ah, ah! Such a hammering! Just here! Oh, oh!

MRS. H. Poor papa! (*Coming to him.*)

BAR. (*walks up and down*). Don't pity me. Call your mamma.

MRS. H. Yes, papa; and I'll get some ice to put on it, too. (*EXIT*, R. 1 D.)

HOL. (*advances to* BARGISS). I'm awfully sorry about that head — where did you get it?

BAR. Sh! Don't say anything. I haven't got a headache.

HOL. Why — what?   [GASLEIGH *gets around to* R.

BAR. I have the utmost confidence in your discretion, Paul. (*Takes his hand.*) And so I want to whisper that it's a little *ruse* to enable me to go out this evening with the Professor.

HOL. (*assuming an air of severity*). Ahem, papa! (*Shakes his head.*)

BAR. (L.). What do you mean, sir, by shaking your head? It's what Dickens did. They all do it.

HOL. (*coolly*). Where are you going?

BAR. (*whispers*). To the Academy.

GASLEIGH (*whispers*). Behind the scenes.

HOL. (C., *brightening*). No! Can you get behind the scenes?

BAR. Yes; as a supernumerary. I'm to be disguised as a high priest.

GAS. (R.). Yes. A high priest in the opera.

HOL. Oh!

BAR. As you are going to stay at home to-night, you can keep Hypatia quiet while I'm gone.

HOL. (*serious*). No, I can't do it.

BAR. Why not?

HOL. I will not assist in a plot to deceive my wife's mother. (*Stage*, R.)

[*READY* MRS. BARGISS, *to enter* R. I D.

BAR. Then you'll betray me?

HOL. No, sir. I'll go with you. (*Back to* C.)

BAR. (*staggers against piano, sits down and stares at him;* GASLEIGH *also.*) You — what?

HOL. (*crosses to him*). Now, don't become excited, papa. If you go, I go.

BAR. (L.). Have I warmed a serpent?

[*READY* JESSIE, *with folded napkins and some cracked ice in a bowl, to enter* L. C.

HOL. (C.). It's my duty to watch over you.

BAR. (*starts up*). You go behind the scenes in a promiscuous gathering? Suppose you should be recognized?

HOL. I will go also as a high priest. (*To* GASLEIGH.) I suppose there's more than one?

GAS. (R.). You can take my place. I was to be a conspirator.

HOL. The very thing. Just in my line. As a conspirator, I'm unequalled. I believe it requires the hat pulled down — the cloak drawn tightly — thus — the dagger grasped in the right hand — and a hoarse laugh in three syllables. Ha, ha, ha! How's that? (*Crosses to* R.)

GAS. Capital.

[BARGISS *and* HOLLYHOCK *stride across to* R. *All laugh heartily, particularly* BARGISS, *who suddenly breaks into a groan at sight of* MRS. BARGISS.

ENTER MRS. BARGISS, R. I D.

Mrs. Bargiss. Why, my darling — I didn't know you had a headache. Dora has just gone for some ice.

Bar. (*gruffly*). Of course I've got a headache. I always have a headache when I'm put out.

Mrs. B. (*gently*). It isn't my fault this time.

Bar. I didn't say it was, did I? Oh, my head, my head! (*Up and down stage L.*)

ENTER Jessie, l. c., *with napkins folded, and cracked ice in bowl.*

Jessie. Here's the ice, sir. (*EXIT, l. c.*)

Mrs. B. I'll put on the bandage directly. Have a little patience.

Bar. That won't help it. (*Goes up and pushes her hand away.*)

Mrs. B. Well, I never! (*Goes to ice.*)

Hol. (*suddenly puts hand to his head, and walks up and down r.*) Oh! O — o — h!

Mrs. B. Have you a headache, too?

Hol. Ever since dinner, and it's growing worse every minute. Oh! Oh!

Bar. Oh! Oh! Such a hammering at the back of my head. (*Up and down.*)

Hol. Mine's right in front. (*Up and down.*)

Mrs. B. (*bringing down an iced cloth*). Do let me put this on.

Bar. You may — it won't do any good. [*She ties it on.* Oh! Oh! The cold water's running down my back!

Hol. I'll try one, but it'll only make me worse, I know. (*Goes to table and puts one on, assisted by* Gasleigh.)

Gas. (l. *of divan, putting bandage round* Hollyhock's *forehead*). There's nothing like rest for a headache. Quiet and undisturbed rest. Let me suggest that you lie down for a few hours.

Bar. (*meekly*). Do you think it would do me good?

MRS. B. Of course it will. Go, dear, at once.

BAR. I'll lie on the sofa in the study.

HOL. I'll go with you. It's the only place I'm sure of quiet. Oh! Oh! My poor head! (*EXIT*, L.)

BAR. (*to* MRS. BARGISS, *who assists him*). Don't let any one come near me — on any account. Oh! Oh! My head! (*As he goes* L., *he winks and shakes his foot at* GAS-LEIGH. *EXIT*, L. D.)

MRS. B. Poor Launcelot! He never had such a head-ache before. I do think I ought to sit by him and bathe his temples. (*Resolute, and about to go after him.*) I will.

GAS. (*coughing slightly*). Ahem!

MRS. B. (*turns. He makes a sign of silence to her*). What is it?

GAS. Something for you. (*Taps his breast pocket.*) A little surprise.

MRS. B. I'm getting a good many surprises to-day.

GAS. The "Sonnets to a Fiancée" are out.

MRS. B. At last?

GAS. They'll be on sale at every bookstore .o-morrow. What do you think of it? (*Produces a red cloth bound book, gilt-edged, and gilt sides and back.*) This is the first copy struck off and bound. Permit the humble printer to present it to the esteemed patron, in honor of the gifted author.

MRS. B. (L.). Oh, how kind of you, Professor! And Bargiss suspects nothing?

GAS. Nothing.

MRS. B. (*shakes his hand*). And the binding is so rich. (*Crosses to* R.)

GAS. It — a — cost — a little more than the estimate.

MRS. B. I'll pay it cheerfully. (*Opens book and reads title.*) "Sonnets to a Fiancée, by Launcelot Bargiss." (*Crosses to* R.)

GAS. (*takes his hat*). My dear madam. I see that you

would be alone with this memento of your happiest years. Allow me to take my leave.

[*READY* JESSIE, *with student-lamp, to enter* L. C.

MRS. B.   Oh — a — Professor — there's another little thing. We must get the book noticed well, you know. Will you see that the critics are put in good humor?

GAS. (*strides to her; folds his arms*).   Madam, you touch me on a sore spot.   Against the gigantic monopoly of modern criticism — against the critics' ring I have set my face. We are going to crush it.

MRS. B. (R.).   How?

GAS.   We are going to have the authors criticise their own works.   It will be the triumph of the 19th century over the customs of the past.   (*EXIT*, L. C.)

[*READY* FLOSSY, *with book, to enter* R. C.

MRS. B. (*comes down, turning over the pages*).   How pretty they do look in print!   With every one comes a memory. This came after his first bouquet.   (*Recites.*)

> "I sent thee late a rosy wreath,
> Not so much honoring thee,
> As giving it a hope that there
> It might not withered be."

(*Speaks.*)   And this came enclosed with the invitation to a picnic.   (*Recites.*)

> "When daisies pied and violets blue,
> And lady-smocks all silver white,
> Do paint the meadows with delight."

Ah !   (*Closes book with a sigh as* JESSIE *ENTERS*, L. C., *bringing in a student-lamp, not lighted, which she places on table* C., *and lowers the window-shade* L.

It will be a grand surprise for Launcelot at breakfast tomorrow. I'll put the volume under his napkin. He'll discover it — he'll read all his little sonnets in print — and it will be the sensation of his life.

[*READY* Mrs. Hollyhock, *with letter, to enter* R. 3 D.

JESSIE (*timidly*, L.). Please 'm, I've a favor to ask of you.

MRS. B. What is it, Jessie?

JES. I'd like to ask if I could go to the Private Coachman's ball to-night, ma'am.

MRS. B. Certainly not. You know this is Betty's night

ENTER FLOSSY, *with book*, R. C.

off and, besides, Mr. Bargiss is ill. If anything happened, I wouldn't have a person to send with a message.

JES. (*begins to cry*). I never have any time off.

MRS. B. You can go some other night.

JES. Some other night won't be the Private Coachman's ball. (*EXIT*, L. C.)

[FLOSSY *puts book on table, and looks for another.*

MRS. B. What are you doing, Florence?

FLOSSY. I'm getting something to read. (*Selects a book and brings it down.*)

[MRS. BARGISS *takes it out of her hand, as a matter of course, and looks at the title on the back.*

MRS. B. "La Bruyère's Characters!" (*Hands it back to* FLOSSY.) That's the book Mr. Corliss recommends so highly.

FLOS. (*confused*). Is it? I had forgotten. (*Turns leaves over and sits on divan.*)

ENTER MRS. HOLLYHOCK, R. 3 D., *with a letter.*

MRS. HOLLYHOCK. Where is Paul — does any one know?

MRS. B. (C.). In the study, with papa.

[MRS. HOLLYHOCK *about to go.*

You mustn't disturb them. They are both suffering from headache. [*READY* JESSIE, *to enter* L. C.

MRS. H. (R.)   No wonder, with the life we are leading. (*Shows letter.*)   Here's a letter from home.   It's written by Jobbins to *me*.

MRS. B.   To you?

MRS. H. (*crosses to* L.)   Yes.   He has written eight times to Paul and got no answer.   Everything's at sixes and sevens on the farm.

MRS. B. (*takes letter and glances over it*).   It's too bad.   I told you he wasn't the husband for you, Dora.   You'll bear me out that I warned you against that man.   (*Hands letter back.*)   When Flossy's turn comes, I'll have a little more of my own way.   (*Stage* R.)

[*READY* TAMBORINI, *to enter* L. C.

FLOS. (*comic despair*, C.).   Oh, mamma, I sha'n't trouble you for a long time yet.   (*Puts her book on table*, C.)

MRS. B. (R., *affectionately stroking her chin*).   We don't know, child.   We don't know.   I may have something to say to you soon.

FLOS. (*starting*).   Mamma !

MRS. B. (*soothingly*).   Oh, it's nothing yet.

ENTER JESSIE, *at* L. C., *and savagely.*

JESSIE.   Signor Tamborini wants to know if you are at home.

MRS. B. (*crosses to* JESSIE).   What kind of a tone is that to speak to me ?   Show Mr. Tamborini up instantly.

[JESSIE *flings herself out*, L. C.

That girl has been ruined by the city.   All this because she can't go to the Private Coachman's ball.   (*Changing tone and smiling mysteriously.*)   Florence, I think you had better not be present when Signor Tamborini delivers his message.

FLOS. (R. *quickly and seriously*).   Mamma — has this visit any connection with what you have just hinted to me ?

MRS. B.   Perhaps, darling — perhaps.

FLOS. (*hotly*). Oh, mamma! Pray don't think of Lord Lawntennis. I couldn't — never, never! (*EXIT*, R. C.)

MRS. B. We'll see when his lordship offers himself.

ENTER TAMBORINI, L. C.

TAMBORINI. Oh, Signora! I haf been so fortunate as to secure the box for you for the new opera to-morrow that you wanted. There will be a great crowd. Immense success — splendid. They haf a full dress rehearsal this evening. I just come from there.

MRS. B. Thank you, Signor. My daughter's husband will be greatly obliged.

TAM. Oh, the tickets are for your son-in-law?

MRS. B. Yes.

TAM. Then I might as well have handed them to him on the stage before I came away.

MRS. B. (R.). Handed him — on the — stage?

MRS. H. (L.). Mr. Hollyhock?

TAM. *Ma si.* Yes. I just saw him there. He is one brigand — one bandit. He is a — (*gesture of eating soup*) he is a — supe!

MRS. B. } (*together*). What?
MRS. H. } My husband?

TAM. (*aside — taps left elbow with his right hand, while his left is held to forehead; crosses to* R.). I make one blunder. His wife and moder not know he is out.

MRS. H. Mother! My husband on the stage! Behind the scenes! I'll go there this minute. I'll see for myself. (*Rushes up for her cloak.*) I'll drag him home, costume and all.

[*READY* JESSIE, *with* MRS. BARGISS'S *cloak and hat, to enter* L. C.

MRS. B. (*following her*). Dora, you will do nothing of the kind. A man like that is not to be run after. He is to be despised. (*Very vigorously.*)

Mrs. H. (L., *tearfully*).   I do despise him — but I want to see him with my own eyes.   (*Gets cloak.*)

Mrs. B.   No, no.   I'll send your father.   He is the proper person to take care of my gentleman.

Tam.   Is that so?   Ah, then, it is all right.   Mr. Bargiss can take care of him.   He is there, too.   He is one high priest.   (*Describes flowing beard, etc.*)

Mrs. B. (*screams*).   What?   Bargiss?   My husband, too! (*Touches bell furiously.*)   Jessie!   (*Up* c.)   Jessie!   My cloak and hat!   (*Furious.*)

Tam.   I make one oder mistake.   (*Renews pantomime of tapping elbow.*)

Mrs. H.   It's an outrage — an insult.   (*She walks to and fro.*)   [*Rain and lightning.*

Mrs. B.   Signor Tamborini, will you conduct my daughter and myself to that place instantly?   (*To* Mrs. Hollyhock.) We'll drag them home just as we find 'em.   [*Rain.*

Tam.   But, Signora, it is raining.   [*Loud storm.* It is great storm.

ENTER Jessie, L. c., *with* Mrs. Bargiss's *cloak and hat, which she helps her to put on.*

Mrs. B.   No matter.   I'd go through floods and deluges.

Tam.   But how shall I get you in there?   I know not.

Mrs. B.   You'll find a way.   (*Suddenly bringing him front.*)   Signor!   You are seeking the original of that por- · trait.   I'll show her to you to-morrow if you take us on that stage to-night.

Tam. (*with fire*).   With that promise, Signora, you may twist me round your leetle finger.   (*Gesture.*)   Come! [*The storm is very furious.*

Mrs. B. (*going up*).   Now, then, Dora.   We'll take a carriage.

Mrs. H. (*going up*).   Now, then, mamma.

--

Tam.   There will be a tableau on that stage to-night.

[*EXEUNT* l. c.

Jessie.   Well, What's up now! All of 'em running head first to the theatre.   She don't seem to be frightened as much as she was about the old gentleman's illness.   Perhaps he's better.   I guess they won't miss me if I run down to the ball for an hour.   (*Peeps in at room,* r. c.)   Miss Flossy's there.   (*Looks towards door* l.)   And the gentlemen are in there.   (*Turns chandelier down : stage half dark.*)   I'll just have one dance, and get home before they get back.   (*EXIT,* l. c.)

The noises of the rain are very strong, with flashes of lightning and distant thunder.   The stage is deserted a few seconds. Then the door of Flossy's *room opens, and she ENTERS with a little shaded lamp, lighted.*

[*READY* Postman, *with bag, to enter* l. c.

Flossy.   Where did I leave my book?

[*Violent gust of wind and rain.   Shutters slam.*

(*She starts, frightened.*)   Oh, what a flash!   I had it here. (*Finds book on table.*)   Ah, here it is.   What a storm!   It's enough to frighten one.   I always did tremble at a storm. (*Goes to window, raises the shade a little and peeps out.*) Ugh!   What weather!   I pity any one who has to go out. (*Looks across street.*)   He's at home.   At least there's a light in his room.   How I hate a man that never goes out, but walks up and down in his room like a polar bear in his cage.   He comes to his window.   He looks across.   (*Angry, pulls shade down.*)   What business has he to be staring across!   (*Peeps cautiously through corner of shade.*)   That's another of his impertinences.   I ·wonder how he'd like to have anyone staring across at him !

[*Front door-bell rings.   Lightning.*

Now he leaves the window.   Oh, dear, I hope he didn't notice my peeping over !   [*Bell again.   Rain and wind.*

I wouldn't have that for the world. He's just capable of
suspecting that I peeped on his account.

[*Bell again. Lightning. Storm ceases.*
Who can be ringing so? Is Jessie deaf? (*Goes to* c. *and
calls.*) Jessie! Jessie! She seems to be out. (*Goes out
*L. C. *and presently returns after calling* "Jessie" *outside.*)
She's actually gone out. I suppose I must open the door
myself.   [*Bell again.*
I'm coming! (*EXIT*, L. C.)

Returns immediately, followed by a one-armed veteran POSTMAN
with a bag. He is dripping wet — rubber cape, etc.

POSTMAN. (L.). Well, young lady, you let me ring long
enough.

FLOS. I don't know where our girl has gone.

POSTM. Letter for Hollyhock — Paul. (*Hands it.*) Nothing else.

FLOS. You are very wet. Wouldn't you like to go down
to the fire?

POSTM. (*in doorway*). Thank you, young lady. I haven't
time. But I am dripping like a sponge. There's two cents
due on the letter. It's short one stamp.

[*Lightning and rain.*
FLOS. I'll get it for you. (*Goes to* R. U. E.) Paul!
(*Knocks.*) Paul!

POSTM. What weather! (*Wrings his hat.*)

FLOS. (*opens door and looks in* R). Nobody there. (*Rec-
ollecting.*) Oh — he's with papa. (*Crosses and opens door
*L.) Not there, either. (*Exit* L., *calling.*) Papa — Paul!
(*Re-enters, showing some alarm.*) Where are they all?
(*Runs down to* R. I E.) Mamma! (*Exit, calling* "Mamma
— Dora;" *re-enters, more alarmed.*) Mamma! Where are
you? Nobody here? Good heavens, there's nobody at
home! I'm alone in the house!

POSTM. (*smiles — in doorway*). Well, no matter. I'll collect it next time. I must be off. (*Going.*)

FLOS. (*pulling him back*). Oh, you mustn't go. I can't be left here all alone.

POSTM. But, young lady —

FLOS. (*bringing him down — terrified*). Please,— please don't desert me. I'll die of fright. I'm all alone in the house.

POSTM. (*soothingly*). But it's not so bad, not so bad. It's true something did happen in this house once.

[FLOS *screams and hides her face in his cape.* There was a man found under the bed, I think.

FLOS. (*screams and clings to him*). Oh, oh, oh! You must stay. I won't let you go.

POSTM. (*gently releases himself*). You've got your hands all wet. I'll dry them in my handkerchief. (*Does so.*) I'm really very sorry for you, but I can't stay, you see. I'm only a postman, and I have to get through my round.

FLOS. But what shall I do? I can't stay in this house, and I can't run out in the street alone.

POSTM. Isn't there anyone you can call in?

FLOS. Not a soul. (*Crossing R.*)

POSTM. None of the neighbors?

FLOS. (*crosses to L.*) Neighbors? (*Sudden thought; runs to window joyfully.*) Yes, he's there. He would come — I know he would. (*Eagerly to* POSTMAN.) He lives across the way. He'd come if I'd ask him.

POSTM. (*going up*). I'll go and tell him.

FLOS. (*On his R., catching him by the cape*). Oh, oh, oh! (*Shuddering.*) Don't leave me — don't leave me! We'll bring him over. Help me to light all those candles. No, I'll light them in front of the window. Why didn't I think of him at first!

[*Talks through bus. of lighting all the candelabra and handing them to* POSTMAN *to place in window.*

*She lights the first and gives it to him, telling him
to light the others, and during her speech gives time
for him to do so. He lights those on mantel. She
brings the one she lights from* c. *of* l. *table, then
meets* POSTMAN *coming down with another, which
he gives to her, and gets the other off the mantel.*

He's so good — so honest — so noble-hearted. You know
he's a relation of ours — the gentleman across the way.

POSTM. (*bringing down candelabrum*). Yes, miss.

FLOS. Now I'll raise the shade. So. He must notice
this. He'll wonder what I do it for. (*Crosses to* L.) Now,
you stand right here. (*Places him in front of window.*) And
keep beckoning. So. (*Shows him.*) You see? So. Take
something in your hand — something white — a large paper.
(*Sees play-bill on divan.*) This will do — what is it? (*Looks.*)
Oh, this will be splendid. "Come Here." "Leah, the
Forsaken" — that'll bring him. (*Folds it so as to show the
words* "Forsaken. Come Here.") Now, hold it up so.
(*She holds it on the man's breast, standing behind him, and he
beckons for* CORLISS *to come over.*)

POSTM. There's some one at the window.

FLOS. (*eagerly*). Where? (*Looks.*) It's he. He looks
out. He throws up his window. He nods. He waves his
hand. (*Laughs in glee and claps her hands almost hysteric-
ally.*) He's coming! He's coming! (*Crossing* L.) Now
we can put out all the lights. (*When lights are out all but
one.*) I'm so glad!

POSTM. (*puts bill on divan*). Now I may go —

FLOS. Oh, yes. I'm not at all afraid, now.

POSTM. — and attend to Uncle Sam's business.

FLOS. (*dips down in her pocket*). There, that's for you.
And with all my thanks, besides.

[*READY* CORLISS, *with hat and overcoat, to enter* L. C.

POSTM. Thank you, miss. I'm a father, too, and got
gals of my own. Nothing but gals. Some folks they say,

"oh, for a boy;" but, for me, I say nothing goes to a man's heart like a daughter — a true, good daughter. Good-bye, miss, good-bye. I'll let the gentleman in.

FLOS. (*suddenly*). Don't say anything to him. I mean, don't tell him anything.

POSTM. (*nods and smiles*). All right. I won't.

[*Bell heard.*

There he is. Good-bye, miss, good-bye. (*EXIT*, L. C.)

[*Music.*

FLOS. (*realizing her situation*). But what shall *I* tell him? I can't say that I was scared, like a baby. But I must say something. What will he think? What have I done? It's awful to be alone with him — and so late at night.

CORLISS (*heard outside in a cheery tone*). Thank you. Very good. I'll go up.

FLOS. (*listens*). He's coming! My heart's in my mouth. (*Looks around helplessly.*) What shall I do? (*Looks at door* R. I E.) Ah! That's it. (*Runs to door and opens it about a foot. She holds her hand on the knob.*)

ENTER CORLISS, L. C. *Throws his overcoat on chair and places his hat on it — then comes down.*

CORLISS. Did I understand rightly, Miss Florence — you called me?

FLOS. (R., *whispers*). Sh! Not so loud. Mamma! (*Indicates room* R.)

COR. (*not comprehending*). I beg pardon.

FLOS. (*whispers*). In there! She's lying down on the lounge. She's had such an awful attack of — something.

COR. (*softly*). I'm very sorry.

FLOS. (*speaks off to an imaginary Mamma*). Mamma! Mr. Corliss is here now. (*Comes forward, leaving the door open.*) You must forgive me for calling you over, but I really didn't know what else to do. We were alone — and all of a sudden mamma was taken. I sent the girl to the drug store — but if she gets worse, some one must go for a doctor. Mamma thought you'd be angry at being sent for —

Cor. (*goes quickly towards door* R.). I'm entirely at your service, my dear mad— [Flossy *prevents him going further.*

Flos. And I thought you might be angry, too — after the way we parted this evening.

Cor. (*offers his hand*). Let us forget it.

Flos. (*takes hand warmly*). Agreed. (*Suddenly withdraws.*) Mamma and I thank you ever so much for coming.

Cor. It's not worth mentioning. (*Again towards door.*) I only regret, my dear madam, the occasion is such a sad one.

Flos. (*draws him away gently by the arm*). Sh! Don't speak so loudly. She has a dreadful headache. Here's the cracked ice! (*Up to table* C.)

[Corliss *gets round to* L. *of table.* I got it for her. I'm going to make her a fresh bandage. (*Stands* R. *of table ; he* L.)   [*They speak in subdued tones.*

Cor. Can't I help you? I know how to nurse people.

Flos. How did you learn?

Cor. On the plains. You didn't know I'd been in the army?

Flos. Were you?   [*They work at ice and bandages.*

Cor. Yes. I'm an old West Pointer. Had my little service with the redskins.

Flos. Did you fight the Indians?

Cor. A little.

Flos. I saw from the very first that you had a military air. You are so bold.

Cor. No. I'm a great coward.

Flos. What — really?

Cor. Judge for yourself. I wanted to win a girl's heart. I found it occupied, and I retreated without striking a blow.

Flos. (*innocently*). You mean she loved another?

COR. No. The enemy in possession was a little contemptible imp we call a whim — a caprice — an obstinate coquetry — that I ought to have charged and routed at the first.

FLOS. (*confused*). You believe her as bad as that?

COR. That's as bad as a good, pure, lovable girl can be. Her heart should be as open as the day. I thought to find *hers* so.

FLOS. (*shy, yet curious*). Did you love her?

COR. (*warmly but gently*). I love her yet.

FLOS. Was she handsome?

COR. (*warmer, yet subdued*). How can I describe her? Her eyes looked into my very soul, and its chords were stirred by the voice from her laughing mouth as the harp is stirred by the touch of the player. You see — I tremble even as I think of her.

FLOS. (*rises, and softly*). Was she good?

COR. (*roguishly*). Between you and me, she was a little good-for-nothing flirt — but a charming little flirt for all that.

FLOS. (*one step away*). And it's all over — forever?

COR. It is over. She fluttered away from me like a butterfly — or like a thoughtless child sporting in a meadow. But if I could catch her — could hold her for one moment pressed to my heart — her eyes riveted on mine — I could whisper such eloquence in her ear that her heart should answer with an echo of my love. (*Tries to take her in his arms.*)

FLOS. (*evading him, pretends to listen*). Sh! Mamma!

COR. Did she speak?

FLOS. (*confused*). I think she called me. I'll take the ice in to her. (*Takes napkin with ice and pretends to go in room* R., *but stands behind door so audience can see her.*)

COR. (*kisses his hand after her*). Oh, you delicious little — I think I need some ice myself. (*Ties a bandage around his head.*)

FLOS. (*behind the door, holding the bandage to her head*). I'm all in a glow. How refreshing this is! If my heart didn't beat so! I'm actually afraid he'll hear it thump.

COR. (*applies ice to his pulses*). It must be the lights that make it so hot. (*Blows out the remaining candelabra.*)

[*Stage half dark.*

FLOS. (*while he is blowing out the lights*). He loves me! He really loves me! I could cry out with happiness. But he mustn't make love to me now. Not to-night. (*Suddenly alarmed.*) It's getting dark. What has become of the lights? (*Comes out.*) What are you doing, Mr. Corliss?

COR. (*pulling his bandage off, confused*). I — I — was merely putting out some of the lights — I thought they made it too — too —warm for your mother.

FLOS. (*goes to chandelier and pulls cord. It lights up*). Oh, no. Mamma is much better. (*With intention.*) We needn't speak so low any more.

COR. But it was so pleasant.

FLOS. No, no. Mamma asks as a particular favor that you speak quite loudly.

COR. It's the worst thing in the world for a head-ache.

FLOS. (*loudly*). She likes to hear us talk. It entertains her. (*Takes up play-bill.*) Did you ever see these plays?

COR. (*angrily*). No — yes — of course.

FLOS. Are they good?

COR. (*struck with an idea*). Have you never seen them? (*Takes bill from her.*)

FLOS. Never.

COR. Oh, the love-scenes are magnificent.

FLOS. Do tell me about them.

COR. Leah stands there — as you do — her lover approaches (*steps towards her*) to urge his passion in glowing words. [FLOSSY *turns away.*
She listens to him with averted head and downcast eyes.

(*With fire.*) Oh, look at me — give me one glance to bid me hope — to say you love me !

FLOS. (*starting up, and in fear*). Why, Mr. Corliss !

[*READY* MRS. BARGISS *and* MRS. HOLLYHOCK, *to enter* L. C.

COR. (*recollecting himself, crosses to* R. *and speaks off*). That's in the play. Oh, I recollect every word of it. (*To* FLOSSY.) He sees her blush — then tremble — then, unable longer to restrain himself, he takes her hand. (*He seizes* FLOSSY's *hand.*) He presses it to his lips. (*Does so.*) It's the play, you know. (*Tenderly.*) Then, with gentle yet passionate words, he beseeches her to answer and tell him that she loves him.

[*READY* BARGISS, HOLLYHOCK, *and* TAMBORINI, *to enter* L. C.

FLOS. (*turns her head to him and gives him her other hand also*). There !

COR. (*clasps her in his arms*). My darling — my own !

FLOS. Is that in the play, too ?

COR. Yes — that's the best of it.

FLOS. (*breaks away and runs to door* L. C.). Heavens, I heard the door close. Some one is coming. (*Throws a kiss to* CORLISS, *and at door,* R. C.) I can't stay. Good-bye ! Good-bye !

COR. (*tries to call her back*). Florence ! (*Comes down, jubilant.*) She's mine ! (*Stops as he glances at door* R., *and remembers Mamma.*) Heavens, her mother has heard everything ! (*In a nervous whisper to audience.*) Well — all I've got to do is to go right on. Why not get her consent at once ? (*Buttons up his coat resolutely and goes to half-open door ; bows and speaks off.*) Madam — as you have heard all — my avowal to your daughter — the declaration of a passion which knows no bounds —

[*Here* MRS. BARGISS *and* MRS. HOLLYHOCK *appear* L. C., *and stand in doorway.*

— and whicn dates from the moment I first beheld her picture. I have no excuse to make for approaching you at this moment with the favor I have now to ask —

[*READY curtain.*

MRS. BARGISS. What's that? (*Makes a step forward.*)

COR. Eh? (*Turns; sees* MRS. BARGISS.) By jove — my boomerang.

[*Darts up* C. *and is met by the apparition,* L. C., *of* BARGISS *and* HOLLYHOCK, *in costume, urged in by* TAMBORINI.

BARGISS. Boomerang, eh? Look at this!

[*RING curtain.*

TABLEAU AND CURTAIN.

ACT IV.

SCENE. — Same as in Act. III.

TIME. — Morning. ENTER JESSIE, L. C., *with card on salver and humming the "*Iolanthe*" Galop. Trips forward with an imaginary partner. READY to enter,* MRS. BARGISS, R. I D. ; TAMBORINI, *with bouquet,* L. C.

JESSIE. Well, I got off this time all right. Miss Florence promised not to tell that I stole off and left her all alone. She says she wasn't a bit frightened — she had her thoughts to keep her company. I'd rather have one of those private coachmen to keep me company. (*Dances and hums the galop again until she reaches* MRS. BARGISS's *door,* R., *and knocks.*) Here's Signor Tamborini's card, ma'am. He's waiting.

ENTER MRS. BARGISS, R. I D., *severe but calm. She takes the card.*

MRS. BARGISS. Show Signor Tamborini up.

JES. Yes'm.

MRS. B. Where is Mr. Bargiss ?

JES. In his study ma'am, with Mr. Hollyhock.

MRS. B. Very good. You can go.

[JESSIE *starts off in a galop.*

Jessie !

[JESSIE *subsides and EXIT,* L. C.

I believe I have the requisite firmness to dispose of those gentlemen this morning. (*Sits at desk* L. *to write.*) For one of them, at least, the time has come.

ENTER TAMBORINI, L. C., *in evening dress as usual, carrying a superb bouquet.*

TAMBORINI.   Signora !

MRS. B. (c.).   You are determined to lose no time, Sig.
nor Tamborini.

TAM. (R.).   As soon as I leave you last night, I tele.
graph to his lordship that the lady in the picture is found,
and that I learn her name to-day.   His lordship he tele.
graph back instanter.   *Voilà.*   (*Hands despatch.*)

MRS. B. (*crosses to* R., *reading*).   " Place at the feet of the
Signora the loveliest of bouquets, and my profuse acknowl.
edgments."

TAM. (*handing bouquet*).   Signora, with the profuse acknowledgments of my Lord Lawntennis.

MRS. B. (*takes bouquet; reads on*).   "When you have
learned the name of the fair original, telegraph me at once,
that I may communicate directly with her."   (*Gives back
telegram and smells bouquet.*)   His lordship is exceedingly
polite.

TAM. (*produces note-book*).   And now, madame—the name
and address of the young lady.   I telegraph in your own
words.   [*READY* BARGISS *and* HOLLYHOCK, *to enter* L. D.

MRS. B.   Prepare yourself for a surprise, Signor.   The
young lady you are seeking is my daughter Florence.

TAM. (*surprised*).   Your daughter?   *Da Vera ! Ma dio
mio !*   The Signorina *Fiorenza* has the hair of gold, while
the young lady of the picture is black on the top.   (*Gesture.*)

MRS. B.   That is easily explained.   The artist took the
liberty of changing her hair.

TAM. (*suspiciously*).   Wait one moment.   (*Cunningly.*)
In the picture there is one large, immense, big dog.   (*Gesture.*)

MRS. B.   Our mastiff, Max.   You can see him at our
place in the country whenever you please.

TAM. (*delighted, and writing*).   Then it is all right.   Ah,
Signora, my heart is breaking out with joy.   I telegraph at
once.   His lordship will break out with joy, too.   (*Pantomime*

of suitor in ecstasy — struck by picture and asking hand.) All is well — I fly — I telegraph. (*Bows himself half up the stage.*) Signora, *Illustrissima !* Signora — *Ornamentissima !* (*EXIT,* L. C.)

MRS. B. (*rising*). That affair is properly inaugurated. I'll see that it is properly terminated. I'll have my way this time. (*Goes up* R.)

ENTER BARGISS *and* HOLLYHOCK, L. D.

HOLLYHOCK (*peeping in*). The coast is clear. (*Coming forward.*)

BARGISS (*peeping in*). Are you sure? (*Coming forward.*)

HOL. (*turns, and sees* MRS. BARGISS, *who turns and glares at both*). I — I — I —

BAR. Oh, Lord! (*Stands hiding behind* HOLLYHOCK *like a schoolboy.*)

[MRS. BARGISS *stands a moment measuring them with her glance; then sails down* R.

BAR. (*nudging* HOLLYHOCK). Say something. Go for her.

HOL. (*advancing timidly, and in a plaintive voice*). Mamma, mamma!

MRS. B. (*turning*). What is your business with me, sir?

HOL. I have a particular favor to ask, mamma.

BAR. (*timidly*). So have I, Hypatia.

MRS. B. (*crosses to* BARGISS). You and I will have an understanding, by and by. (*To* HOLLYHOCK.) What do you wish, sir?

HOL. (R.). I would like to see my wife, if it's not inconvenient.

MRS. B. (C.). Indeed! Pray, do you think it necessary to ask my permission to speak with your wife?

HOL. Yes, mamma.

MRS. B. Undeceive yourself, sir. I will announce your presence to my daughter myself. (*Goes to door up stage,* R., *and knocks.*)

BAR. Now, my darling! (*Taps her on the shoulder. She looks at him freezingly. He starts away alarmed, staggers over to desk* L., *and buries his face in the papers.*)

MRS. B. (*knocking again. Calls icily*). Dora!

MRS. H. (*partly opening door,* R. 3 E.). What, mamma.

MRS. B. The person whom your father selected for your husband wishes to see you.

> [MRS. HOLLYHOCK *slams the door and a bolt is heard to shoot.*

You hear that?

HOL. (C.). What was it?

MRS. B. My daughter has bolted her door on the inside. That is your answer.

> [*READY* MRS. HOLLYHOCK, *to enter* R. 3 E.

HOL. (*crosses to* R.; *goes resolutely to door*). With your permission, I will see about that.

MRS. B. You will find she has a strength of character inherited from her mother (*a piercing glance at* BARGISS, *who groans and writhes in his chair*), impervious to persuasion.

BAR. Oh!

HOL. (*coolly*). What is she going to do?

MRS. B. Remain a prisoner while she is compelled to stay under the same roof with you.

HOL. (*with mock emotion*). Then all is over?

MRS. B. (*going up* C.). All.

BAR. (*beseechingly*). Hypatia!

MRS. B. (*quickly*). What, sir?

BAR. (*groans*). Nothing! (*Buries his face in his hands at desk* L.)

MRS. B. All that is over. (*EXIT,* L. C.)

HOL. (*who has stood crushed until she is out of hearing, returns quickly to the door and calls*). Dora! (*Knocks.*) Dora, it is I — she's gone.

> [MRS. HOLLYHOCK *opens the door and peeps out, smiling.*

MRS. HOLLYHOCK. Are you sure?

HOL. Yes.

MRS. H. (*bounding into his arms*). Dear Paul !

HOL. My sweet, good wife !

BAR. (*at desk, astonished*). How did you manage that? I wish you'd tell me the way.

HOL. (c.). We made it up last night. Didn't we, darling? (*Kisses her.*) I wouldn't let her go to sleep with a single suspicion or misgiving.

BAR. (L., *advancing*). My wife wouldn't let me put in a word. I never passed such a Polar night.

MRS. H. (*to* BARGISS). Mamma mustn't know we are reconciled, just yet. (*Crosses to* c.) She worked on me so, that I made a solemn promise to despise Paul.

[*READY* MRS. BARGISS, *with letter, to enter* L. C.

HOL. But I wouldn't be despised, would I? (*Kisses her.*)

BAR. Don't you know she may come back at any moment?

MRS. H. Then you must watch out for us.

BAR. What will they do with me next? What a draught there is in this place ! (*Goes up, wraps a shawl over his head and shoulders, and sits at door,* L. C., *the picture of misery.*)

HOL. (*embracing her*). Now we are safe.

MRS. H. You act just as if nothing had happened

HOL. Nothing particular has happened. It was only one folly. That young man is a wizard. My time came to_ make a fool of myself, and I did it. I shied my little boomerang, and it came back on me.

MRS. H. And you will never again?

HOL. Never again. (*Kisses her.*)

BAR. (*suddenly*). She's coming.

[HOLLYHOCK *and* MRS. HOLLYHOCK *separate. He runs to door* L. *She to door* R. *They conceal themselves.*

HOL. (*just over the threshold*). I say, Dora.

MRS. H. (*the same*). Yes, Paul.

BAR. Here she is. [*They both close their doors.*

MRS. BARGISS *sails in,* L. C., *and passes* BARGISS, *who makes a mute appeal. She goes to the desk and puts a letter which she has brought into an envelope, and addresses it.* BARGISS *comes down to her after some hesitation.*

BAR. My darling!

MRS. BARGISS (*at desk, not looking at him*). I wish to give you notice that after to-day you must take your meals at a hotel.

BAR. But, Hypatia—

MRS. B. I leave for home, with my children, this evening.

BAR. What's to become of me?

MRS. B. You will be free to pursue your literary studies and collect your materials wherever and whenever you please. (*Crosses to* R.) My duty is to spare my children the disgrace of seeing their father degrade himself and them.

BAR. Now what have I done?

MRS. B. (*sobbing*). And to think this should happen on the very day I had promised myself so much happiness! When I had such a surprise in store for you!

BAR. Don't, Hypatia! You make me crawl.

MRS. B. (*producing the book of sonnets*). Here, take it. My pleasure is spoiled, anyway.

BAR. (*examining cover of book*). What is this?

[MRS. BARGISS *turns away, sobbing and wiping her eyes.* HOLLYHOCK *opens his door and takes a step or two out, but sees* MRS. BARGISS *and retreats.*

HOLLYHOCK. O Lord!

BAR. (*puts on spectacles and reads*). "Sonnets to a Fiancée, by Launcelot Bargiss." (*Looks at her.*) Sonnets? What sonnets?

Mrs. B. (*occasional sobs*). They are poems you sent me when we were engaged.

Bar. (L.). Heavens! You had those things printed under my name?

[*READY* Corliss, *with hat, to enter* L. C.

Mrs. B. Yes. In secret, to give you a surprise. They are now for sale all over the city.

Bar. (*reels to chair*, L.). Woman! It's all over; I am lost.

Mrs. B. (*startled*, C.). Why so? What is the matter?

Bar. Those things are not mine.

Mrs. B. Not yours?

Bar. They were selections from Shakespeare, Jonson, Tennyson, Byron, Scott, everybody.

Mrs. B. Then you deceived me even at that happy period

Bar. Deceived you? Confound it, don't everybody quote poetry when they're in love. Who'd ever dream that you'd send that infernal collection to a printer, and put my name to it. Now I am done for.

Mrs. B. Launcelot! I meant it for the best.

Bar. Oh, you've done it for the worst. I shall be the laughing-stock of the city. (*Jumps up*.) Where's my coat and hat?

Mrs. B. Where are you going?

Bar. To the bookstores, to the printer's, to the news-stands, to the type-founders, to stop them.

[*She helps him on with hat and coat as*

Corliss *ENTERS*, L. C.

Corliss. Ah! there you are. I'm most fortunate — if I may have the pleasure of a few minutes —

Bar. Excuse me. I'm busy! Talk to my wife. Where can I get a cab?

Cor. But —

Bar. Can't attend to anything now. I'm boomeranged. (*EXIT*, L. C.)

[MRS. BARGISS *totters down and sinks into a chair.*
HOLLYHOCK *makes a few steps out as before. Retreats again.*

MRS. B. (L.).   Oh, if he's only in time !

[*READY* FLOSSY, *to enter* R. I D.

COR. (*observing all this with a puzzled air, now approaches*
MRS. BARGISS, *hat in hand, somewhat embarrassed*).   My dear
madam, I owe you an apology for the unceremonious and
abrupt manner in which I took my departure last night.

MRS. B. (*who has recovered, rises from desk*).   I think we
had better not refer to last night's performances.

[CORLISS *hides his head in his hat.*

Still, as I presume you have come here to repeat your proposal for my daughter in a respectable manner, you are
entitled to a serious answer.   That answer is — No !   Under
no circumstances — No !

COR. (*quickly*).   Madam !

MRS. B.   Enough, sir.   (*Crosses to* R.)   I have other views
for Florence, and I shall not permit them to be interfered
with by any person.

COR.   Very well, madam.   Very well.   But I have rea-
sons for not relinquishing my hopes.

MRS. B.   Indeed !   I suppose you think my daughter may
have ideas on the subject different from mine.   I'll con-
vince you of the contrary very soon.   (*Goes to door*, R. H.,
and calls.)   Florence, step here a moment.

COR. (*aside*, L.).   That's all I want.

ENTER FLOSSY, R. I D.

FLOSSY.   Here I am, mamma.   (*Starts on seeing* CORLISS.)
You didn't tell me —

MRS. B.   My dear, this gentleman has proposed for your
hand.

FLOS. (*lowering her eyes*).   Indeed !

MRS. B. (C.). I have informed him that I have other plans regarding you.

[FLOSSY *makes a gesture of entreaty, aside.*

And I am resolved to select my second son-in-law myself. I believe I informed you of this last night, and you acquiesced. Is this true?

FLOS. (*eyes on floor*). Yes, mamma.

[HOLLYHOCK *and* MRS. HOLLYHOCK *steal out of
their respective rooms and exchange eager signs with
each other.* MRS. HOLLYHOCK *points warningly
to her mother.*

MRS. B. And yet Mr. Corliss thought he might be able to test your filial duty in a personal interview.

FLOS. (*pretending severity*). I will never do anything mamma does not approve of, Mr. Corliss. (*Crosses to him.*)

HOLLYHOCK (*eagerly, across to his wife*). I must tell you something.

[MRS. BARGISS *overhears him, and turns to the side
he is on.* MRS. HOLLYHOCK *flies back to her room.*

MRS. B. What are you doing here? (*Goes up and looks
off* L.)

HOL. I, oh, oh, nothing. (*Goes towards his room.*)

FLOS. (*quickly to* CORLISS, *while her mother's back is turned*). I'm only pretending. I'm on your side. (*Crowding him
into corner.*)

COR. My angel!

MRS. B. (*turns and interrupts them. They resume positions*). My eldest daughter, Mr. Corliss, married against my advice. Look at the result.

[*The moment* MRS. BARGISS *has turned down the
stage,* MRS. HOLLYHOCK *and* HOLLYHOCK *embrace,
c., and kiss at the end of* MRS. BARGISS'S *speech.
She does not look.*

COR. (C.; *turns, back to audience; looks up stage; beholds
the embrace*). The result is horrible! Horrible!

MRS. B.   Is it not?   Here are two married people separated, perhaps forever.   Had she listened — had she taken my advice —

> [MRS. HOLLYHOCK *is struggling to get away from* HOLLYHOCK'S *arms.*

FLOS.   Don't excite yourself, mamma.   I'm going to be good.   (*She darts to window and looks out, snatching a rose from vase,* L.)

MRS. B.   You are my only comfort.   While your sister — (*Turns slowly up stage.*)

> [HOLLYHOCK *and* MRS. HOLLYHOCK *separate.   He walks up stage dejectedly.   She flings herself into a chair — eying him scornfully.*

COR. (*crosses to* FLOSSY.   *Kisses her hand*).   Won't you give me that rose?

FLOS. (L.).   I can't.   Mamma is watching.

> [*READY* BARGISS *and* JESSIE, *with basket of books, to enter* L. C.

COR.   Do, now quick.

> [*She is about to give it.*   MRS. BARGISS *having reached* MRS. HOLLYHOCK'S *side,* CORLISS *and* FLOSSY *fly apart.*

MRS. B.   I will not blame you, Dora.   You are doing your duty.   Come to my heart, my poor, deceived child. (*Draws her to her side.*)   Flossy!   (*Tenderly.*)

> [FLOSSY *goes to her mother, hiding the rose in her hand.*

This is a sad day for a mother, my children.   We have only ourselves to lean upon and look up to.   (*She is* C. *of group.*)

> [FLOSSY *gives* CORLISS *the rose.   He kisses her hand.* HOLLYHOCK *kisses* MRS. HOLLYHOCK'S *hand on the other side.*

(*She comes down, releasing her daughters to the gentlemen, but not observing the fact.*)   And now, gentlemen, we will not detain you any longer.   My daughters have been brought

up to obey their parents — or to speak more properly at the
present time — one of their parents — and that one — (*She
turns near the door.*)

> [*The groups fly apart into different positions.*
> HOLLYHOCK *throws himself into a chair up stage,*
> R. FLOSSY *into chair,* L. C. MRS. HOLLYHOCK,
> R. C. CORLISS *at piano,* L.

That one is their mother. (*EXIT,* R. I D.)

> [*All resume group.*

HOL. Mamma is sublime.

MRS. H. For shame, Paul!

> [*He embraces her as they go up.*

FLOS. (*shaking her head as she comes forward with* COR-
LISS). No. Arguments avail nothing for the present.
Leave it to me. I'll win her over by degrees.

COR. I'm sure you will. (*Hugging her in rapture.*) You
darling!   [MRS. BARGISS *reappears in door.*

MRS. BARGISS. Florence!

FLOS. Yes, mamma. (*Sails into room after* MRS. BAR-
GISS, *and kisses her hand to* CORLISS *as she gets to door.*)

> [MRS. HOLLYHOCK, *meanwhile, has flown to her
> room, with* HOLLYHOCK *before her.*

COR. Victory! Victory!

> [*Goes up waving his hat, and meets*
> BARGISS *who ENTERS, with* JESSIE, L. C. *They bring in
> a huge clothes-basket laden with books,* "Sonnets to a
> Fiancée."

BARGISS. Set it down here. Now, go down to the wagon
and bring up the rest. Put 'em all in my study.

> [*EXIT* JESSIE, L. C.

(BARGISS *takes off his hat and overcoat; wipes perspiration
from his brow.*) Thank heaven, I stopped them before they
left the binder's.   [*READY* GASLEIGH, *to enter* L. C.

COR. What have you been buying?

BAR. (*getting* C.). My complete works. The whole

edition. (*Takes* CORLISS's *hand.*) My young friend, your words have come true. I have made a fool of myself. Not once, but half a dozen times. It's just as you said. The boomerang has come back on me.

RE-ENTER MRS. BARGISS, R. 1 D.

MRS. BARGISS (*anxiously*). Were you in time?

BAR. Yes, fortunately they hadn't gone out yet. (*Crosses to* C. ; *wipes his forehead.*) I've had a pleasant afternoon of it.

MRS. B. (R., *soothing*). Then there's no harm done.

BAR. Not much. Though I'm done. But my eyes are open at last. I'm done with poetry.

MRS. B. But your society novel?

BAR. We'll light the fire with it.

MRS. B. (R.). And your other works?

BAR. Rubbish.

MRS. B. And your play?

BAR. We'll keep that, and I'll read it to you when we get back to the country. (*Turns away to* L. C.)

ENTER GASLEIGH, L. C., *with a jubilant hooray.*

GASLEIGH. Victoria! Victoria! My friend, let me embrace you. The deed is done. The day is won. My dear madam, I bring you something like news.

BAR. (L. C., *interrupts him, pointing to* CORLISS). You remember what our young friend said about making an ass of one's self?

GAS. (*crosses to* CORLISS). Our young boomerang friend — oh, yes.

MRS. B. What's the news?

GAS. (*crosses to* MRS. BARGISS). The " Sonnets to a Fiancée " have met with a gigantic success — had an immense sale already — immense.

BAR. No!

GAS. I have just come from the printers, and they tell me the whole edition was sold out an hour ago. A single buyer took the whole lot.

BAR. Quite correct. I bought it. There it is. (*Pointing to basket and books.*)

GAS. You? (*Crosses to* L. C.)

BAR. Who else would pay good money for such rubbish?

GAS. Rubbish?

BAR. You've printed under my name a selection of the best things from Shakespeare, Tennyson, Byron, Scott, and all the stars in the literary firmament.

COR. I say, Gasleigh. (*Crosses to* GASLEIGH.) Boomerang. (*Laughs quietly.*)

GAS. You were right, young man. You were right. I've done it, too. (*Sinks into chair,* R. C.)

BAR. And the "Scattered Leaflets"?

GAS. (*calmly, but heroically*). Are scattered forever.

MRS. B. How's that?

GAS. My theories were fallacious. We were simply exposing vanity and mediocrity to public scorn. (*Starting up.*) We must take the other track. (*Confidentially.*) I have an idea. Let us start a paper to crush the amateur poets — the poetical ring. We'll call it the "Waste Basket," and put 'em all in it.

BAR. (*edging off*). I'll take one copy for a week, and longer, if it lasts. But as for literature, I'm done. My epitaph shall be — gone to meet so many more. (*Goes up to* MRS. BARGISS, R. C.) Neat, eh?

GAS. Then, ha, ha, ha! You give up. I'm sorry to lose you. You wrote good enough poetry for me, my good friend. "National Bank. Pay to the order of. Three hundred dollars." Those are the words that stir all men's souls. Well, by-by. No other way, eh?

BAR. (R. C.). Only one way. The way out.

GAS. Ha, ha ! Very good. Very good. Well, so long.
Good-by, Shakespeare. (*EXIT*, L. C.)

BAR. Good-by, sweetheart, good-by. (*To* CORLISS.) I
believe I am thoroughly recovered from my flight of folly,
and capable of taking a common-sense view of the commonplace world. What was it you wanted to say to me as I was
going out a while ago ? (*Puts his hand affectionately on* COR-
LISS'S *shoulder.*)

COR. Oh, I had merely come to ask for the hand of your
daughter.

> [*READY to enter*, JESSIE, L. C. ; FLOSSY, R. I D. ;
> HOLLYHOCK *and* MRS. HOLLYHOCK, R. 3 E. ; TAM-
> BORINI, *with sealed telegram*, L. C.

BAR. (C., *gravely*). Did you speak to her mother ?

MRS. B. (R.). He did — and I felt it my duty to decline.
I have nothing against Mr. Corliss, but I have other views
for Florence. (*With emphasis.*) The happiness of my
daughter is concerned, and I mean to see that we make
(*looking at* CORLISS) no blunder about that.

BAR. (*aside to* CORLISS, L.). That sounds bad. What do
you think of it ?

COR. (*aside to* BARGISS). I think she is casting her little
boomerang.

BAR. It's all nonsense. (*To* MRS. BARGISS.) What have
you got in hand, now ? No more surprises, I hope.

MRS. B. (*knowingly*). Perhaps, my dear.

BAR. What is it ?

MRS. B. I can whisper this much. If I can't be the wife
of a poet, I may be the mother-in-law of an earl.

BAR. Hypatia Victoria Bargiss ! The events of the
morning have unsettled your reason. What earl ?

MRS. B. Lord Lawntennis has seen Florence's portrait,
and intends to make her his wife.

ENTER JESSIE, L. C.

JESSIE. Mr. Tamborini, ma'am. May he come up?

ENTER FLOSSY, R. I D. HOLLYHOCK *and* MRS. HOLLY-HOCK *steal on*, R. 3 D.

MRS. B. Let him enter. (*To* FLOSSY.) Ah, my child.

ENTER TAMBORINI, L. C., *waving a sealed telegram over his head jubilantly.*

TAMBORINI. Signora, it is come. (*Suddenly sees others and bows.*) Signorine! Signori! (*Resuming jubilation.*) It is here. The answer — the message.

MRS. B. (*crosses to* TAMBORINI). From his lordship? For me?

TAM. *Si*, Signora.

MRS. B. (*putting on glasses and opening it*). Let me see.

COR. (*gets beside* FLOSSY, R. C.). You'll stand by me?

FLOS. (R.). If there were a thousand lords against us.

MRS. B. (*has read the telegram; screams, crumples it up, and falls into a chair*). Oh! Oh!

ALL. What is it?

[MRS. BARGISS *starts up and throws the telegram on the floor.* BARGISS *picks it up and smooths it out.*

TAM. (*following* MRS. BARGISS *up and down*). But, Signora! What is the matter?

MRS. B. (*fiercely*). Out of my sight, reptile.

TAM. (*recoils*). *Diavalo! Ma dio mio!*

BAR. (*having read the telegram, blows his nose, replaces handkerchief, and crosses to* CORLISS). I guess you can have her. (*To* MRS. BARGISS.) Can't he, my dear?

MRS. B. (*laying her head on* BARGISS's *shoulder*). O Launcelot! I am ashamed of myself.

BAR. (*soothingly*). There, there. No harm. It was — ahem — only another proof that our young friend was right. We all make fools of ourselves sooner or later. Your turn came rather late. (*Gives telegram to* FLOSSY.) You may like to read his lordship's proposal, my love. (*Gives telegram, and crosses to* R.)

> [MRS. BARGISS *gets next to him.* FLOSSY *getting* C.,
>   *followed by* CORLISS. TAMBORINI *all ears.*

FLOS. (*reads*). "Dear madam : — If the portrait number 728 was that of your daughter, pardon this means of communication, and permit me to make you an offer. If the dog in the picture is for sale, I'll pay you whatever price you name for him. Lawntennis."

TAM. Vat is dat? De tog ! Oh, ciel ! I kill myself. O Signorini, I kill myself. (*Throws himself at the feet of* FLOSSY, *and in pantomime gives himself several imaginary stabs; then bounds up.*) I will not live. I will die. Oh, oh ! (*Doubles himself up on chair at back and remains stupefied till end.*)

FLOS. (*to* CORLISS). Will you have me now? You know I'm not such a prize, after being jilted by an earl.

COR. Let his lordship have the dog. I take the lady, if she'll take me.

FLOS. Take you !

> "If in the works of nature you would find
>   Eternal fitness, women should be kind."

COR. (*taking her hand*).

> And yet how many play a tyrant's part,
>   Betray a worshipper, or break a heart,
>   With gracious flattery will turn and bend
>   To court a stranger, yet will kill a friend.

[*READY curtain.*

FLOS. (*to audience; her hand lingering in that of* CORLISS).

> Dear girlhood friends,
>   We'll be not like them ! Though we cannot choose,
>   But some must sue whose suit we must refuse ;

So base a pride let none upon us prove,
As craves a hundred lovers — not one love.
Wear for your jewel, 'tis a friend's advice,
Not a string of pebbles, but one gem of price.
Fear not to marry one who loves, for know,
Tho' woman be not perfect, love is so.

                [RING curtain

CURTAIN.

COMEDIES AND DRAMAS

JOSIAH'S COURTSHIP — PRICE 25 CENTS
Comedy in 4 acts, by H. C. Dale. 7 males, 4 females. Easily staged. Time, 2 hours. Recommended to dramatic clubs in want of something with good comedy feature and forceful but not too heavy straight business.

THE LAST CHANCE — PRICE 25 CENTS
Comedy in 2 acts, by A. E. Bailey. 2 males, 12 females. 1 interior. Time, 1½ hours. Full of action, bright and witty dialogue, incidentally introducing a burlesque on "Lord Ullin's Daughter." For schools and colleges.

A LEGAL PUZZLE — PRICE 25 CENTS
Farce comedy in 3 acts, by W. A. Tremayne. 7 males, 5 females. 3 interiors. Time, 2½ hours. This play can be highly recommended, the scenes are easy, the dialogue brisk and snappy, and the action rapid.

LODGERS TAKEN IN — PRICE 25 CENTS
Comedy in 3 acts, by L. C. Tees. 6 males, 4 females. 1 interior. Time, 2½ hours. A husband with a strong case of the "green-eyed monster" taking a trip abroad, places his home in charge of a ne'er-do-well nephew. The nephew rents the rooms to tenants, whose diversified characters present great opportunity for comedy acting. This is adapted from the same work upon which Wm. Gillette's famous "All the Comforts of Home" is based.

MISTRESS OF ST. IVES — PRICE 25 CENTS
Drama of the new South in 3 acts, by G. V. May. 7 males, 5 females. 1 interior. Time, 2½ hours. The cast has a typical southern planter of olden times, his two daughters, a peppery southern major, a lawyer from the North, a comical colored valet, etc., etc.

NEVER AGAIN — PRICE 25 CENTS
Farce in 3 acts, by A. E. Wills. 7 males, 5 females. 1 interior. Time, 2½ hours. Fletcher, a crabbed husband, refuses a reference to Dora, a discharged maid. In Marie, the new maid, he discovers an attractive dancer to whom he had been very attentive at a recent ball; the schemes devised by the two maids to punish Fletcher lead to many amusing complications and to an unusual climax.

PETER PIPER'S TROUBLES — PRICE 25 CENTS
Comedy in 4 acts, by J. H. Slater. 5 males, 3 females. 2 interiors. Time, 2¼ hours. The troubles are caused largely by his desire to oblige his friends and are of a social, financial and business variety, all of which are finally overcome.

PHYLLIS'S INHERITANCE — PRICE 25 CENTS
Comedy in 3 acts, by F. H. Bernard. 6 males, 9 females. 1 interior, 1 exterior. Time, 2 hours. Phyllis, Philip's wife, is to inherit a fortune from an East Indian uncle, provided she marries his adopted son, who is about to visit her. Two men call with introductory letters, which she does not read, supposing each in turn to be the adopted son.

A RUNAWAY COUPLE — PRICE 25 CENTS
Farce in 2 acts, by W. A. Tremayne. 4 males, 4 females. 1 interior. Time, 2 hours. A married man of nervous temperament, temporarily in charge of an eloping lady, while the husband-to-be is procuring the license, is himself accused of having run away with her. The arrival of the absent lover relieves the situation and leads to an unusually effective climax.

TOO MANY HUSBANDS — PRICE 25 CENTS
Farce in 2 acts, by A. E. Wills. 8 males, 4 females. 1 interior. Time, 2 hours. The action is continuous, dialogue snappy and climax so unexpected, that this farce can be recommended as one of the most laughable.